He's ba...

There was a moment of panic. We all hit the floor and covered our heads as another shot rang out. With my face pressed against the glass bottom of the boat, I had an excellent view of several brightly colored angelfish drifting by beneath us, their gently waving fins showing their complete lack of concern for the predicament of the humans up top. I could feel Bess shaking beside me and hear the sound of Sydney sobbing.

Now what? I thought desperately, casting my mind around for something to do. *Should we dive into the water and try to swim away? Or—*

"Oh, no!" Sydney sat up. "Look—they hit both our pontoons!"

I gasped, realizing she was right. Those shots had been no accident.

It was difficult to tell which direction the shots had come from—based on where the holes had appeared in those pontoons, I was pretty sure the shooter had been somewhere in the thick jungle off beyond the beach to the north.

I scanned the shoreline in that direction. I squinted toward a jumble of large boulders. Had something moved behind there, or was it my imagination?

nation? ...ed to tell from h... an innocent hil...

NANCY DREW

#1 Without a Trace
#2 A Race Against Time
#3 False Notes
#4 High Risk
#5 Lights, Camera ...
#6 Action!
#7 The Stolen Relic
#8 The Scarlet Macaw Scandal
#9 Secret of the Spa
#10 Uncivil Acts
#11 Riverboat Ruse
#12 Stop the Clock
#13 Trade Wind Danger
#14 Bad Times, Big Crimes
#15 Framed
#16 Dangerous Plays
#17 En Garde
#18 Pit of Vipers
#19 The Orchid Thief

#20 Getting Burned
#21 Close Encounters
#22 Dressed to Steal
#23 Troubled Waters
#24 Murder on the Set
#25 Trails of Treachery
#26 Fishing for Clues
#27 Intruder
#28 Mardi Gras Masquerade
#29 The Stolen Bones
#30 Pagent Perfect Crime
#31 Perfect Cover
#32 Perfect Escape
#33 Secret Identity
#34 Identity Theft
#35 Identity Revealed
#36 Model Crime
#37 Model Menace

Available from Aladdin

CAROLYN KEENE

NANCY DREW

GIRL DETECTIVE®

Model Suspect

#38

Aladdin

New York London Toronto Sydney

❧ALADDIN

An imprint of Simon & Schuster Children's Publishing Division

1230 Avenue of the Americas, New York, NY 10020

First Aladdin paperback edition October 2009

Text copyright © 2009 by Simon & Schuster, Inc.

All rights reserved, including the right of reproduction in whole or in part in any form.

ALADDIN is a trademark of Simon & Schuster, Inc., and related logo is a registered trademark of Simon & Schuster, Inc.

NANCY DREW, NANCY DREW: GIRL DETECTIVE, ALADDIN PAPERBACKS, and related logo are registered trademarks of Simon & Schuster, Inc.

For information about special discounts for bulk purchases, please contact Simon & Schuster Special Sales at 1-866-506-1949 or business@simonandschuster.com.

The Simon & Schuster Speakers Bureau can bring authors to your live event. For more information or to book an event contact the Simon & Schuster Speakers Bureau at 1-866-248-3049 or visit our website at www.simonspeakers.com.

The text of this book was set in Bembo.

Manufactured in the United States of America

10 9 8 7 6 5 4 3 2 1

Library of Congress Control Number 2008943893

ISBN 978-1-4169-7841-1

ISBN 978-1-4169-9688-0 (eBook)

Contents

1	Beachy Keen	1
2	Smile! You're On Camera	16
3	Fire and Water	27
4	Danger in the Water	40
5	Finny Business	49
6	Safe House	54
7	Burning Questions	68
8	Shadows, Sacrifices, and Suspicions	85
9	It's a Jungle Out There	99
10	Dead Ends and Discussions	113
11	Unpleasant Surprises	122
12	Questions and Answers	136

BEACHY KEEN

"So this is what it feels like to live the lifestyle of the rich and famous," Bess Marvin said, peering out the airplane window.

Leaning over from my seat next to her, I glanced out and saw a tiny, lush island ringed with white sand beaches. The midday sunlight sparkled off the azure waters of the Caribbean, making me squint.

On my other side, George Fayne let out a snort. "Yeah, right," she muttered, twisting and wriggling in her seat in an attempt to find a comfortable position for her long, jeans-clad legs. "I'm sure the rich and famous don't have to travel in coach."

Bess rolled her eyes, and I laughed. Bess and

George are cousins and my lifelong best friends. But any possible resemblance ends there. Bess is what you might call a glass-half-full kind of girl. She has a sunny nature to match her sunny blond hair, and prefers to see the best in people until they force her to do otherwise. George, on the other hand, can be a little too quick to see the dark side of any situation.

"Don't complain," Bess told her cousin. "We're just lucky Sydney wants all three of us to come down and investigate this latest trouble instead of only Nancy. After all, she's the real sleuth in this bunch and everyone knows it."

I smiled at the disgruntled look on George's face. "Don't be silly," I told both of them. "The Nancy Drew Detective Agency would be nothing without the little people who've supported me all these years."

I was just kidding around and they both knew it. I don't really have a detective agency. However, I *am* pretty well-known around our hometown of River Heights for solving crimes now and then. And it's true that I probably couldn't have figured out most of them without help from Bess and George.

And it was a good thing I had their help now. Because the mystery we were facing looked like a seriously tricky one.

It all started when Bess and George's other cousin,

Sydney Marvin, had gotten engaged. Sydney was a few years older than us and had a successful career as a fashion model in New York City. Her fiancé—now husband of a few days—was Vic Valdez, the star of a previous season of the hit reality TV show *Daredevils*. The two of them were blissfully in love and had been eager to get married.

However, things went wrong almost from the moment they'd announced their engagement. First Sydney received a series of threatening e-mails. The police in New York investigated but didn't come up with anything. And things had only gotten worse from there.

"I still can't help wondering," I mused now, speaking more to myself than to my friends, "why would anyone want to keep a happy couple from getting married and starting a life together?"

"Who knows?" George retorted. "Why do murderers kill people? Why do arsonists start fires? People are weird."

Bess shot her cousin a look. "Very helpful," she said. "There are lots of reasons someone might want to mess up Syd and Vic's wedding—and now their honeymoon, too. That's practically all we've been talking about for the past couple of weeks, remember?"

"True enough," I agreed, glancing down at my lap as the seat belt sign pinged on overhead. "And

3

we came up with tons of motives and suspects. But that was when we were back home in River Heights with the entire wedding party to work with, not to mention the TV crew. . . ."

Oh, right. That was another thing. When Sydney and Vic became engaged, the two of them had struck a compromise regarding their wedding plans. Sydney got to hold the wedding in her hometown of River Heights, just as she'd always dreamed, instead of in New York City where they both lived. In exchange, *Daredevils* got to film the whole thing. The producers wanted to create a special about the wedding to include as a DVD extra and on their website, and Vic was pretty sure the extra exposure would help him launch his career in show biz. So when the happy couple had arrived in River Heights, they'd been accompanied by an entire entourage consisting of the film crew, several other *Daredevils* cast members, and assorted others.

That was pretty much where my friends and I had come in. Sydney asked all three of us to be bridesmaids. That meant we had a front-row seat for everything that came next. Like watching Vic almost take a sip of jet-fuel–laced punch. And seeing threatening e-mails and texts come in to Sydney's phone on an almost daily basis. And all kinds of other trouble, from mixed-up deliveries to a swarm of biting ants.

It wasn't until the day of Sydney's bridal shower that I'd finally figured out who was behind most of the trouble—it was Sydney's friend and fellow model, Candy Kaine, who was also a bridesmaid. It turned out that Candy, who had introduced Sydney to Vic, had been jealous of their relationship from the get-go. She admitted to pulling most of the pranks in a last-ditch attempt to break them up so she could grab Vic for herself. However, she'd sworn up and down that she hadn't had anything to do with that dangerous jet fuel incident—or with the original spate of threatening e-mails, either.

With the wedding only a week away at that point, I jumped right back into investigative mode. If Candy was telling the truth, that meant there was still someone out there who thought it was a good idea to try to poison people with jet fuel. And I definitely wanted to find out who it was!

As it turned out, she *was* telling the truth. The trouble had continued, ranging from more threatening messages to dangerous stunts like hiding shards of glass in Vic's cake at the rehearsal dinner. But it wasn't until the day of the wedding ceremony itself that I'd cracked the case—or so I'd thought. Circumstantial evidence had pointed to the mischief being the work of Akinyi, Sydney's best friend, roommate, and fellow model, and Jamal Washburn, Vic's best buddy since childhood. Akinyi and Jamal had been a couple for a while about a year earlier. I'd realized that they were on the verge of getting back together, and a timely story about an old fight between Jamal and Vic and some additional factors had led me to accuse them of being the saboteurs. The police had taken them away, causing them to miss the wedding.

But then, during the ceremony, something else had happened. Pandora Peace, another bridesmaid and former *Daredevils* contestant, had pulled a knife out of her bouquet and advanced toward the happy couple up on the altar. She claimed she was just planning to perform a Native American blessing, but the police hadn't thought much of that excuse—especially after they searched her hotel room and found tons of circumstantial evidence implying that she'd been behind most of the other recent pranks as well. They dragged her off to jail, though she protested all the while that she was innocent.

And so the case had seemed—finally!—to be closed. *Seemed* being the operative word. Because the next thing we knew, a mysterious message had arrived from London. It included a copy of the *Daredevils* contract, with one particular clause highlighted. That clause specified that contestants couldn't have any current or prior connection to anyone involved in the production of the show. At the top was a note:

HERE ARE SOME THINGS YOU SHOULD KNOW. THE WRONG PERSON IS IN JAIL. THE CROOK IS STILL OUT THERE! YOU HAVE TO DO SOMETHING. SINCERELY, A CONCERNED CITIZEN

Pretty mysterious, right? Well, not really. See, I'd already figured out that Pandora was involved in a secret romance with Dragon, a current *Daredevils* contestant who was a groomsman in the wedding. There was no return name on the envelope, but I was pretty sure Dragon had sent it, trying to clear his girlfriend's name without destroying his chances on the show.

Given everything that had happened, that might not have convinced me on its own. But then I got an urgent e-mail from Sydney. At that point she was already on her honeymoon on the tiny, idyllic island of Cayo de Oro, where *Daredevils* had arranged a private, superluxe honeymoon for her and Vic. The message had included a photo of a trashed hotel room with a threatening message written on the wall in blood red—ENJOY BEING NEWLYWEDS. YOU WON'T BOTH BE ALIVE FOR LONG! There had also been an attachment with e-tickets for me, Bess, and George, and a plea from Sydney to come down and solve this latest mystery.

So here we were, beginning our descent into the

Cayo de Oro airport. "So do you think this new vandalism is connected with everything that happened back in River Heights?" Bess asked.

"I don't know. But either way, we're sort of starting fresh with our suspect list," I pointed out. "Without the TV crew or the wedding party around, who's left?"

"Vic?" George suggested. "I mean, other than Syd herself, that's pretty much who we've got, right?"

Like I said, George is pretty quick to jump to the most cynical conclusion. Still, I was surprised to hear that she continued to harbor suspicions about Sydney's new husband. I'd thought by then we were all convinced that he and Sydney were truly in love. Not to mention that George is a huge fan of *Daredevils* in general and Vic in particular.

But I had to admit she had a point. "I guess he's got to be on the list," I said reluctantly. "It's true that he had the access, and that he could've faked that jet fuel thing to throw people off. . . ."

Bess smoothed out the skirt of her pretty floral sundress. "At least this time we won't have all those TV cameras around complicating things. That should make it a little easier to figure it out." She smiled. "We'll just have to do our best to play the parts of relaxed tourists enjoying some fun in the sun."

"Sounds good to me." George strained against her

lap belt to get a look out the window as the plane banked. "I wonder if they have parasailing here. I've always wanted to try that."

"Focus, guys," I said. "George, do you really think Vic could have done all this stuff?"

Bess frowned, finally seeming to tune in on what her cousin had said. "No way," she said. "Vic loves Sydney—he'd never do anything to hurt her. I can't believe he had anything to do with any of this."

"Then who did?" George argued. "What, do you think Sydney has a secret split personality and her evil half is trying to sabotage her good half?"

Bess rolled her eyes. "Don't be silly," she said. "Anyway, how do we know this new incident has anything to do with what happened before? It could be totally unrelated."

"After that envelope from Dragon?" George shook her head grimly. "Seems pretty unlikely."

"I have to agree with that," I admitted. "But we should keep an open mind, I guess."

The plane banked more steeply, and the captain came on the loudspeaker to say that we'd be on the ground in ten minutes. Another glance out the window showed Cayo de Oro glittering up out of the Caribbean Sea, looming larger and larger. Exactly what were we going to find down there?

★ ★ ★

"Welcome to Cayo de Oro!" cried a large man with a beaming smile on his broad face. "The island where all your dreams come true!"

"Thanks, dude." George shot the guy a sloppy salute as we hurried past toward the luggage carousel. The tiny island airport was charming, from the friendly greeter to the wicker chairs in the waiting room to the soft calypso music playing over the sound system. But we weren't here for that stuff. I was already turning over motives and suspects in my head. Not that I had much to go on in either category. With any luck, maybe things would look more promising once we reached the resort where Sydney and Vic were staying.

Luckily, our luggage turned up quickly. We grabbed it and headed for the exit.

"Syd said she'd send a car," Bess reminded us.

George was looking around. "Yep, and it looks like that's our ride over there," she said, pointing to a short, middle-aged man dressed in navy linen shorts, a white shirt, and sandals. He was holding a hand-lettered sign with our names on it.

We followed the driver through the airport's glass doors. Outside, the tropical heat hit us like a wet paper towel in the face. It was mid-afternoon, and the whole island had a sleepy feel to it. People were lounging at the bus stop across the way, not seeming in much of a hurry; the fronds of the palm trees lining the parking lot swayed gently in a light breeze. A gleaming black stretch limo was parked at the curb. The driver led us toward it and then started busily packing our luggage into the trunk.

"Now, this is more like it," George said approvingly as we climbed into the car's air-conditioned interior. "Looks like maybe we'll finally get to enjoy some of that celebrity lifestyle after all."

The limo *was* awfully nice. The seats were cushy leather, and there were several cold bottles of water and soda resting in a silver ice bucket beside one of the seats. George grabbed a cola right away, while Bess couldn't stop oohing and aahing over the fancy entertainment system.

But I didn't have much interest in any of that. My mind was still clicking along, turning over the facts and questions of the case. Could the vandalism in Sydney's room really be a whole new culprit at work? There didn't seem to be any other likely answer. Not unless we wanted to go with George's new top suspect: Vic.

"Of course, that doesn't mean there couldn't be someone else we don't know about," I murmured, trying hard to come up with any theory that didn't involve Sydney's beloved new husband as the bad guy.

George glanced up from the mini fridge she'd just discovered under the seat. "What was that, Nance?"

I blinked, realizing I was thinking aloud again. "Oh, nothing," I said. "I was just thinking—what if someone from back home followed Vic and Syd here to Cayo de Oro without them knowing about it?"

Bess's blue eyes widened with alarm. "You mean like that MrSilhouette guy?"

That was exactly what I'd been thinking. About a year earlier, Sydney had had some trouble with an Internet stalker who went by the handle MrSilhouette. My friends and I hadn't known anything about it until Sydney had received a cameo necklace—a pendant with a silhouetted head on it—at her bridal shower. As it turned out, Candy had slipped it into the pile of gifts, hoping to make Sydney freak out enough to cancel the wedding. But now I wondered—what if the *real* MrSilhouette was still out there stalking Sydney?

"It seems possible, right?" I settled back in my seat as the driver jumped in up front and started the car. There was a soundproof barrier between the front seat and the rear compartment, so I felt safe continuing our discussion. "What if MrSilhouette has been hanging around this whole time, maybe spying on Sydney and adding to the trouble whenever he gets a chance?"

"Creepy!" Bess commented with a shiver.

George looked skeptical as she unwrapped a package of cashews. "Sounds more like the plot of a movie or something than real life," she said. "Besides, how would someone like that get close enough to plant that jet fuel, or whatever? Security was crazy tight during all the prewedding stuff."

"The only thing Syd knows about MrSilhouette is that he's got this shiny bald head, right?" Bess said thoughtfully. "So he'd stand out in a crowd, at least if he's young."

"We don't know that he's young," I pointed out. "But you're right—one of us probably would have noticed if there was some random bald guy hanging around."

See, that was all Sydney really knew about MrSilhouette. He'd once sent her a single photo of himself taken from behind. It showed nothing other than the back of his bald head.

"What about that bald cameraman, Butch?" Bess said. "He's the only bald person I can think of who was around for most of the mischief—well, at least if you don't count Syd's dad's bald spot."

I nodded thoughtfully. Butch was part of the *Daredevils* camera crew. He was brusque and rude and seemed to have a bad attitude toward most of the people he was filming, including Vic.

"Yeah, except he never seemed to pay any particular attention to Syd one way or the other. Plus he was the one who saved Vic that time his hair caught on fire, remember?" I shrugged. "But I suppose it wouldn't hurt to call the *Daredevils* production office and confirm that Butch has been safely over in London shooting the next season of the show since before Syd and Vic left for the honeymoon."

George didn't seem to be paying attention anymore. She'd rolled down the window on her side and was staring out and ahead.

"Check it out," she said, sounding excited. "I think we're here!"

I glanced out the window just in time to see a beautifully landscaped sign slide past proclaiming that we were entering the Oro Beach Resort. The limo slowed to negotiate the twisting drive leading to a large cluster of thatched buildings surrounded by palms. Manicured garden beds overflowed with riotously blooming tropical shrubs and flowers, and off to one side I could see part of a rolling, grassy golf course.

"Wow, it looks nice," Bess said. "Check out the waterfall!"

"I can't wait to see the beach," George added.

The window between the front and back seats slid open. "Here you are, ladies," the driver announced politely as he guided the car to a smooth halt at the curb in front of the largest thatched building. "Please enjoy your stay on Cayo de Oro."

"Thanks," we chorused.

The driver was already climbing out, probably intending to hurry back and let us out of the car. But I was perfectly capable of opening a car door myself, and was feeling far too impatient to wait. So I reached over, pushed open the door, and hopped out.

"Look this way, Miss Drew," a gruff voice called out.

I blinked, almost stumbling back against the car as a huge TV camera was shoved in my face.

2

SMILE! YOU'RE ON CAMERA

It felt like déjà vu. But it was all too real.

"Huh?" George blurted out as she emerged onto the curb beside me. By now two or three other cameras were pointed our way along with assorted boom mics and such. "What, did we step into the middle of a shoot for the Travel Channel or something? I thought we were done with this kind of thing!"

"I thought so too," I said, staring at the camera operator. The *very familiar* camera operator. "Er, it's Butch, isn't it?" I said to him. "What are you guys doing here?"

"Slow learners, eh? Don't talk to the camera," the

bald cameraman retorted in his usual curt manner.

"Hello, hello!" a new voice broke in breathlessly before I could respond. Turning, I saw another familiar face. It was Donald Hibbard, the efficient but often frantic young man who was the head production assistant from the wedding film crew. He was rushing toward us from the direction of the nearest building, clutching a handful of papers. His skinny, pale legs stuck out from his billowy Bermuda shorts, and a pair of oversize sunglasses were jammed onto his head, almost lost in his mop of sandy hair.

"What's going on?" Bess asked. She'd joined us on the walkway by now. Her hand strayed to her own hair, obviously checking to see if it was camera ready. As usual it looked flawless, just like the rest of her.

"I guess you guys didn't hear," Donald said with an apologetic shrug. "Mr. Eberhart decided we needed to get a bit more footage. After all, we probably won't be able to feature Pandora as much as he was planning, what with her being in jail and all. So Vic and Sydney have graciously agreed to allow us to join them here on the island for the first week of their honeymoon."

"Really?" I traded a glance with my friends. My first thought was that Sydney couldn't be too happy about this. She'd really been looking forward to having the filming finished so she and Vic could relax and enjoy their honeymoon in private.

But my second thought was that this was a very interesting turn of events. It seemed quite a few of our previous suspects might not be out of the picture after all! The possibilities flooded my mind: Hans Eberhart, the director who might be trying to pump up his career. Madge, the foul-tempered assistant director who seemed to have it in for everyone she encountered. Butch, the bald, surly cameraman my friends and I had just finished discussing . . .

Donald quickly explained that we needed to sign a new set of releases for this stage of the filming. We did so as several resort employees appeared to help the limo driver unload our bags from the car.

"So where is Mr. Eberhart?" I asked Donald as I capped my pen and handed back the release. "I'd like to talk to him about something if he's around."

"Oh, Mr. Eberhart didn't come down here himself." Donald tucked the releases under his arm and tossed his bangs out of his eyes, almost dislodging his sunglasses. "He's in London with the rest of the crew—they're shooting the beginning of the new season over there. He sent Madge down here with just a small crew to take care of things."

Just then a neatly dressed woman approached and

pressed something into my hand. "Your things will be waiting for you in your bungalow when you're ready, ladies," she said in a lilting island accent. "In the meantime, please enjoy the resort."

Before any of us could respond, she turned and glided off back into the lobby building. I glanced down and saw that I was now holding a trio of plastic key cards. Handing one each to Bess and George, I pocketed the last one.

Glancing back toward the drive, I saw a uniformed porter in a golf cart whisking our bags off down one of the walkways between the buildings. "Oh," I said. "I guess we should probably go figure out where we're staying."

"I don't think it'll be much of a mystery," Bess said, peering down at her key card. "There's a number printed right on here, and a little map showing where our place is among the others."

We said good-bye to Donald and headed down the walk after the golf cart. I was half expecting the cameraman to follow us, but to my relief he didn't. Instead he shouldered his camera and strolled off in the direction of what appeared to be some kind of open-air restaurant nearby. I guessed my friends and I weren't famous enough to be worth filming more than our entrance.

"Wow," Bess said as we passed between two large

thatched buildings, which appeared to make up the lobby area and a lounge. "This really changes things, doesn't it?"

"Sure does," George agreed. "I guess maybe we haven't lost all our suspects after all—there's Madge, for one. I always thought she was up to no good." She shot me a look. "Plus since Hans Eberhart *isn't* here, it means Nancy can't start suspecting him again."

"Hmm? Oh, right," I said, feeling a little distracted. Eberhart had directed a couple of arty films early in his career, and George was a big fan. She'd been dismayed when I'd put him on my suspect list in the beginning. But it looked like she wouldn't have to worry this time.

"All right, with Eberhart out of the picture, who else have we got?" Bess asked. "There's Madge, like you said."

"Yeah," George agreed. "And what about that Butch guy? Weren't we just saying he could be MrSilhouette?"

"Ssh," I warned them as we emerged into an open area with a gorgeous free-form pool at the center of it. But I didn't have to worry. There was nobody in sight except a resort employee skimming leaves off the surface at the far end of the pool.

The golf cart and our luggage had long since disappeared, but Bess seemed to know where she was going. She strode briskly across the pool area and entered a shaded cobblestone arcade. Small, expensive-looking boutiques lined both sides of the walkway, and wrought-iron benches and potted palms decorated the middle.

"I think it's this way," Bess said. "All the bungalows are right on the water, so if we just head in the direction of the beach, we should be able to find it."

"Why bother?" George pointed out. "They already took our bags there for us. So maybe we should just look for Sydney."

Bess frowned. "We just got off a plane, remember?" she said. "I want to help Syd as much as you do, but I think that can wait for five minutes while we all freshen up."

"Oh, please." George rolled her eyes. "The TV people rented out this whole place for Syd and Vic. It's not like you need to primp in case you meet some cute guy."

Bess frowned. "Maybe *you* don't mind looking like a ghoul on camera, but I happen to think it's worth taking two seconds to try to look human. . . ."

The two of them continued bickering as we drifted along, but I wasn't paying much attention. Halfway down the shopping arcade, George glanced over at me.

"Earth to Nancy," she said, waving a hand in front of my face. "What's the matter?"

I blinked. "Sorry," I said. "I was just thinking about what Donald said."

"Yeah, so why are you looking so glum all of a sudden?" George said. "This is good news, right? Having the film crew here means we're not starting from scratch after all."

"Oh, I know—it's not that." I sighed, feeling uneasy. "It's just that hearing Donald mention Pandora just reminded me again that the wrong person might be in jail—and that I'm at least partially responsible for her being there."

Bess dragged her attention away from the stylish bathing suits on the mannequins outside the nearest shop, which she'd just stopped to admire. She turned to peer into my face as George and I drifted to a halt too.

"Don't you dare beat yourself up about that, Nancy," she told me. "You were just trying to help Syd. Besides, Pandora pulled a big honking knife in the middle of the wedding, remember?"

"Yeah," George put in. "We all thought she was guilty, including the cops. Her being in jail isn't anything like the stuff with Akinyi and Jamal. . . ."

Her voice trailed off. I guess she'd seen me wince.

"Smooth move," Bess chided her. "You just had to remind her of that when she was already feeling guilty, right?"

"It's okay," I said as George started to apologize. "You're right. It's not the same as that at all." I sighed as I thought about that whole mess. "It's probably a good thing the only place I'm likely to see Akinyi again is in one of Bess's fashion magazines," I added ruefully as the three of us started walking again. "She was pretty gracious when I apologized at the reception, but still—she doesn't seem like the forgive-and-forget type."

"Yeah," George agreed.

Bess didn't answer. We'd just reached a spot where the shopping arcade opened up into an open-air seating area. Several coffee shops and food stands stood at each end, and directly ahead we had a stunning view of the large teardrop-shaped lagoon some fifty yards away down a slight hill. As distracted as I was, I had to admit the view was gorgeous. The crystal water sparkled beneath the late-afternoon sunlight, and even from this distance I could make out the shapes of fish swimming around out there. Off to the left stood a cluster of quaint thatched-roof huts on walkways out over the water, and farther down that way was a broad white beach backed up by a tangle of tropical jungle. Out in the ocean beyond the reef that protected the lagoon, several sailboats were taking advantage of the perfect weather.

"Wow," George said. "I take back my complaints

about flying in coach. It was worth it to get here!"

I nodded and glanced over at Bess. To my surprise, I saw that she was staring off to one side of the seating area, ignoring the picture-postcard view. At first I thought she must have been distracted by spotting another fashionable outfit or something. But that wasn't it.

"Hey," she said, pointing. "Isn't that Akinyi over there?"

"Huh?" George turned to look. "What, you mean a picture of her or—oh! Yeah, that's her all right!"

I nodded slowly. There was no mistaking the model's impossibly tall figure, her flawless features, or her gorgeous ebony skin. At the moment Akinyi was draped in a gauzy cover-up over a tiny bikini. She was posing on a wrought-iron bench in front of a colorful blooming shrub while a photographer snapped away. A *Daredevils* cameraman was filming the photo session while Madge, the assistant director, looked on.

"What's she doing here?" George wondered aloud.

I shook my head. At that moment Akinyi turned her head and spotted us. The serene expression on her face soured into one of mild distaste.

"Come on," Bess said. "We might as well go over and say hello."

"Oh, right," Akinyi said as we hurried up to her and the others. "Syd said you three were coming."

Madge shot us an irritated look. "Do you mind?" she snapped. "We're in the middle of something here."

Akinyi tossed her a cool glance. "Actually, I could use a drink of water," she said, sweeping past the assistant director toward one of the nearby food stands. "Let's take five."

For a second Madge looked ready to argue. But I guess even she didn't want to mess with Akinyi. Or maybe being in charge instead of second in command had mellowed her a little. Either way, she just waved one skinny hand in the direction of the cameras and then stomped off with her cell phone pressed to her ear. The photographer shrugged and lowered his camera, though the TV cameraman kept right on filming Akinyi as she grabbed a bottle of water.

"Um, we weren't expecting to see you here," Bess said tactfully as Akinyi took a few gulps of the water.

The model finished drinking and wiped her mouth with the back of one hand. "I know," she said in her lightly accented voice. She had been born somewhere in Africa, though the slight accent and her exotic looks were the only traces of that background. "Syd and Vic flew me and Jamal down here as a way of apologizing for what happened."

I smiled sheepishly. Was it my imagination, or had she shot me a quick look when she'd said that?

"Yeah," I said. "Um, listen, Akinyi, once again I'm really sorry about everything that happened. It's just that when I heard that story about Vic making Jamal lose his job, and then we found the raincoat and stuff in your rooms . . ."

"Never mind." She made a sort of sweeping motion, as if pushing away my apology. "It doesn't matter." She glanced over at the TV camera, which was still rolling. "We needn't speak of it."

I wasn't sure if she meant she didn't want to talk about the incident at all, or just when the camera was filming us. Either way I was happy to let the subject drop.

"So," Bess said to Akinyi, "this resort seems really nice. Have you had a chance to—"

Whatever she was going to ask was cut off by a sudden ear-piercing, high-pitched alarm blasting out of the speakers in the seating area. Along with that came a flurry of slightly muffled yells and screams from somewhere not too far away, topped by one panicky shout that rang out over the rest:

"Fire!"

FIRE AND WATER

"**O**h!" Akinyi exclaimed, clutching at her heart. I forgot to mention one other thing about her. She's one of the most neurotic people I've ever met. Every little thing sends her into a tizzy.

"Come on!" George shouted, springing into action. "Let's go see what's going on!"

We all raced off in the direction of the shouts. Right around the corner from where we were was a huge, open-sided thatched building that I guessed must be the resort's main dining room. It held dozens of rustic wooden tables, large and small, with tropical centerpieces and woven placemats. In the center of the room was what appeared to be a small dance floor. At the moment about a dozen people, most dressed in resort uniforms, were milling around there, and a few puffs of smoke were drifting up toward the high ceiling where they were dissipated quickly by the overhead fans.

"What's going on?" Madge called out, pushing past us to hurry forward.

The crowd parted, revealing a familiar figure—a tall, broad-shouldered guy with a blond buzzcut and a sheepish expression. "Hey look, it's Bo," George commented.

I was a little surprised, though I shouldn't have been. Bo Champion had been one of Vic's *Daredevils* costars and was now one of his closest friends. He'd also been a member of the wedding party. Speaking of parties, Bo was the type of guy who never missed one. It was no wonder he'd decided to tag along to Cayo de Oro, especially now that it seemed half the wedding party was invited. Still, his unexpected presence made me wonder. . . .

"Sorry about that, everyone," Bo called out. He glanced down and stomped on a spark smoldering on the jute rug at his feet. "I was just, uh, showing Lainie here my excellent fire-juggling skills, since she never saw the episode of the show where I did it." He laughed and shrugged. "Guess I'm a little out of practice."

"Figures. He's been showing off for her all week," someone muttered just behind me.

Glancing over my shoulder, I saw that it was the *Daredevils* cameraman who'd been filming Akinyi's photo session. "Really?" I asked him. "You mean Bo likes that girl?" I glanced at the pretty young woman he'd called Lainie, vaguely recognizing her as one of the makeup artists from the production crew. She had a cheerful smile, thick strawberry blond hair, and a distinctive mole on her chin.

The cameraman looked startled, as if he hadn't expected to be overheard. "You didn't hear it from me, all right?" he said. Then he shouldered his camera, hit the on button, and hurried forward to film Bo as he continued to apologize.

"It's okay, Bo," Lainie was saying. She giggled and tossed her lush, shoulder-length hair back over one shoulder. "Your demonstration was very impressive."

Bo grinned back at her, suddenly seeming unaware of the watching crowd. I hid a smile.

"Did you hear what the camera guy said?" I murmured to my friends. "Sounds like we might have a little side romance going on here."

"Cute," Bess declared. "I just hope they're not snagged by that same clause that got Pandora and Dragon in trouble."

"Doubtful," I replied. "I'd have to look at the exact

language again, but I'm thinking that only applies to relationships that existed prior to or during the filming of the season in question. Since Bo's been off the show for over a year now, and is presumably just now getting involved with a crew member, they should be okay."

George laughed. "Spoken like a lawyer's daughter," she joked. "Carson would be proud."

The excitement over, most of the crowd was already drifting away. A couple of employees turned up with brooms and dustpans and began cleaning up the charred remains of whatever it was that Bo had accidentally set on fire, which appeared to be a palm frond from one of the flower arrangements and the corner of a rug.

Just then another familiar figure appeared, this one tall and lanky with a head of short black spikes. "Vic!" Bo called out. "Yo, dude, you missed all the fun."

"I heard." Sydney's husband strode toward his friend, a grin on his thin, handsome face. "Trying to burn down my honeymoon, bro?" He glanced over at Lainie and winked. "Or were you trying to start another kind of fire?"

Lainie blushed. "Excuse me," she said. "I was only supposed to be on a fifteen-minute break. I'd better get back to work."

She hurried off, disappearing around the corner.

"Come on," I told my friends. "Let's go talk to Vic. He probably knows where Syd is."

"Hey there!" Vic greeted us as we approached. "You made it! Thanks so much for coming down— Sydney will be relieved to see you."

"You're welcome." I smiled at him, then turned to Bo. "Long time no see. I didn't know you'd be here."

Bo chuckled. "Hey, I'm always up for a vacation," he said. "When I heard the private honeymoon was turning into a party, I decided to cancel my other plans and fly down."

That was pretty much what I'd just been thinking. Still, I couldn't help wondering if we'd been over-looking Bo as a suspect all along. True, it was hard to imagine Vic's good-natured, easygoing buddy being behind the jet fuel incident or the other terrible stuff that had happened—or what kind of motive he might have for doing any of it, for that matter. On the other hand, he'd been around for most of the mischief, and easily could have pulled most of it off. . . .

"So where's your beautiful bride?" Bess was asking Vic. "We just got here, so we haven't seen her yet."

"She's at the spa." Vic sighed. "Needless to say, she's, uh, a little tense, so she decided to get a massage while she was waiting for you to get here."

I nodded. "So have you figured out anything about what happened?"

"Um, not exactly. I mean, I think Sydney can explain when you see her." Vic glanced over my shoulder.

Looking back that way myself, I saw that Butch and the other cameraman were back there filming away. It figured. Vic probably couldn't so much as poke his nose out of his bungalow without being on camera. After all, he was the star of this show.

At that moment Jamal hurried into the dining hall. "Hey, there you are," he greeted the other two guys. Then he blinked, suddenly noticing my friends and me standing there. "Oh, hello." He shot a slightly nervous glance at the cameramen, then returned his attention to us. "Uh, welcome to Cayo de Oro. Good to see you again."

"Same here," Bess said politely.

It didn't take a detective to see that the guys didn't want to talk about the situation while the cameras were rolling. Neither did I.

"Okay, um, see you later," I said, trying to act casual. "Guess we'll, um, go say hi to Syd, um, now."

What can I say? I'm a detective, not an actress.

Vic glanced at the two cameramen, who appeared to be holding a whispered discussion. I winced, guessing that they were deciding which of them would stay with the guys while the other accompanied us to film our reunion with Sydney. As far as I knew, they had no idea why we were really there. But that wouldn't stop them. I was pretty sure they were under orders to film any encounter with either member of the main couple.

Before I could figure out what to do, Vic spoke up again. "Yo, dudes," he said to Bo and Jamal. "I was just thinking, it'd be fun to play a little game of extreme dodgeball with a coconut instead of a ball." He shot a wicked grin and wink in the direction of the cameras. "Might leave some bruises, but that just makes it easier to tell who won. You guys up for it?"

"You bet!" Bo said immediately.

Jamal laughed. "Come on, V. Let's show him how we play—Jersey style!"

The three of them raced off, whooping and hollering. The cameramen muttered a few more words to each other, shot us an uncertain look, and then rushed off after the three guys.

Whew! I guessed the prospect of getting extra angles on the nutty action of the impromptu game had overruled the potential value of our quiet spa moment with Sydney. That had been quick thinking on Vic's part. He might come across on TV as nothing more than a brainless, attention-starved daredevil, but in real life he had a lot more than that going for him. No wonder Sydney had fallen for the guy.

"Come on, let's get out of here before Madge sends

another camera to follow us," I told my friends.

Bess nodded. "I saw a sign for the spa on our way here—I think it's this way."

It didn't take us long to find the resort's spa. Like most of its lodgings, it was located in one of those private thatched huts on the warren of wooden walkways set out over the lagoon's glassy shallows.

"Wow," George muttered as the three of us entered the plush, carpeted lobby of the spa. "This place is pretty fancy. A little *too* fancy, if you know what I mean."

I knew what she meant. The place was superposh. It takes a lot to intimidate me, but I have to admit I felt kind of underdressed and grubby as I looked around.

Luckily Bess never feels that way, even when she's just disembarked from an international flight. "Excuse me," she said, striding right up to the reception desk. "We're looking for Sydney Marvin—er, Marvin-Valdez. We heard she might be here."

The impeccably dressed woman behind the desk nodded. "Yes, of course," she said. "Ms. Marvin-Valdez is expecting you. Right this way, please."

"You're here!" Sydney sat up straight when we entered her treatment room, almost knocking over the petite young woman who'd been busily massaging her face with some kind of green goo. "Oh, thank goodness! This is such a nightmare. . . ."

"Um, could you excuse us for a second, please?" Bess shot an apologetic glance at the facialist. The young woman nodded and melted away, leaving us alone with Sydney.

There was a flurry of hugs, some of which involved the transfer of Sydney's green facial goo to various bits of our clothing. But even Bess didn't seem to mind that.

"So," I said after a moment, settling back against the woven bamboo countertop beside the massage chair. "What's going on, Syd?"

Sydney shot an anxious look toward the door. "Not here," she whispered, reaching for a tissue and starting to wipe the goo off her face. "These walls are made of paper—pretty much literally. We should find someplace private to talk."

She had a point. The interior walls of the spa appeared to consist mostly of bamboo and paper screens. "Okay," I said. "Should we go to your bungalow?"

Sydney shook her head. "I have a better idea. . . ."

Soon the four of us were drifting on the lagoon's crystal-blue waters. The boat we were in was pretty cool—it was a four-person glass-bottomed paddleboat with big, rubber inflatable pontoons. It made it easy to observe the busy and colorful underwater world of fish and coral.

But I was trying not to get distracted by any of that. We weren't there for a vacation, and I wanted to hear what we were up against. The saboteur had already all but ruined Sydney's bridal shower, bachelorette party, rehearsal dinner, and wedding day. I was going to do all I could to make sure he or she didn't ruin her honeymoon, as well.

"Do you think we're out far enough now?" George panted, allowing her legs to slow on the paddleboat's pedals.

I shot a look back toward shore. Vic and his friends were romping around on the white-sand beach, lobbing coconuts at one another and laughing uproariously. It also appeared they'd set up a boom box to serve as a soundtrack to their game—driving hip-hop music was faintly audible drifting out over the water.

Sydney nodded, seeming satisfied that we wouldn't be overheard. "This is horrible," she blurted out, lifting her feet from the pedals and sort of flopping against the side of one of the pontoons. "I was so looking forward to this honeymoon, but it seems like everything just went wrong from the start!"

It was clear that she was on the verge of tears. Bess reached over and took Sydney's hand in her own.

"Deep breaths," she advised gently. "Just tell us."

Sydney gulped in a lungful of air. "Well, to start with, there was the stuff about the TV crew coming along." She glanced back toward the beach, where Butch and the other camera operator could be seen filming the guys' antics.

"Yeah, we figured that one out right away," George said. "Couldn't you just have said no to that whole plan? It's not your fault Pandora went all wacky—well, wacki*er*—and got herself arrested."

"I suppose." Sydney bit her lip. "But Vic thought it'd be helpful to the production if we went along with it, and it's only for the first week. . . ."

"Never mind," I said, shooting George a look. The last thing we needed at the moment was to get Sydney even more upset! "It's done now. So what happened?"

"I thought Vic and I would at least get some privacy on the flight down," Sydney tapped her fingers nervously on the rubber pontoon beside her. "But the producers insisted on switching us onto the private plane they'd chartered for the crew so they could film on the way down. Then we couldn't even enjoy arriving here in this gorgeous place, since Madge made us disembark from the plane, like, forty times trying to get that right shot. And then did the same thing with getting out of the limo when we got here. . . ."

"Bummer," George said succinctly.

"Anyway, Vic managed to talk them out of filming some kind of carrying-me-over-the-threshold scene after that, since they'd already done that back home at the hotel after the wedding. So we actually got to head over to the bungalow on our own." Sydney drew in a long, shuddering sigh. "But when we got there, we found that mess I sent you in the picture!"

"Don't worry," I said, seeing that her blue eyes were filling with tears once again. "We'll get to the bottom of it. But listen—were Akinyi and Jamal and Bo on that chartered flight too?"

"Bo was," Sydney said. "But not the other two. They ended up taking our original first-class seats on the regular flight—just one more way for us to apologize, you know?" She shrugged. "Anyway, they were lucky. They got here a few hours before we did, so they actually had a chance to enjoy it before the crew arrived."

She shot another sour look toward the cameramen back on shore, giving me a chance to take in what she'd just said. So Akinyi and Jamal had been at the resort for several hours before Sydney, Vic, and the others had arrived. Interesting.

I opened my mouth to ask another question, but I never got the chance. A loud, sharp retort rang out from somewhere in the direction of the shore, echoing off the water and the trees. A second later came the *thunk* of something hitting one of our boat's pontoons.

"Duck!" George cried, diving for the floor. "I think someone's shooting at us!"

DANGER IN THE WATER

There was a moment of panic. We all hit the floor and covered our heads as another shot rang out. With my face pressed against the glass bottom of the boat, I had an excellent view of several brightly colored angelfish drifting by beneath us, their gently waving fins showing their complete lack of concern for the predicament of the humans up top. I could feel Bess shaking beside me and hear the sound of Sydney sobbing.

Now what? I thought desperately, casting my mind around for something to do. *Should we dive into the water and try to swim away? Or—*

"Hey," George said. "Is that it?"

I lifted my head, realizing that at least ten or fifteen seconds had passed and no additional shots had followed those first two. *Was* that it? Had the shots been some kind of accident or something?

"Oh, no!" Sydney sat up. "Look—they hit both our pontoons!"

I gasped, realizing she was right. No, those shots had been no accident.

"Come on." I hoisted myself out over the rapidly shrinking pontoon and kicked off my shoes. The lagoon was fairly shallow, but still a bit too deep to stand up in where we were. "Guess we'd better swim for shore before the shooter decides to come back for more target practice."

Soon all four of us were doggy-paddling toward shore. The water was calm and it was pretty easy going even dressed in the clothes we'd worn on the flight down. "Don't let your feet touch any of the coral," Bess warned us. "Some of it might be poisonous."

"Good point," George said.

I didn't respond. It was difficult to tell which direction the shots had come from—sound carried differently over water than it did over land, especially since the lagoon was basically a big bowl surrounded on three sides by tree-lined slopes leading up to the mountains at the center of the island. But based on where the holes had appeared in those pontoons, I was pretty sure the shooter had been somewhere in the thick jungle off beyond the beach to the north.

As I swam, I scanned the shoreline in that direction. Unfortunately the sun had started to sink toward the horizon and we were swimming almost directly into it, making it tough to see much in the shadowy trees along the shore. I squinted toward a jumble of large boulders. Had something moved behind there, or was it my imagination? Even if it wasn't, how was I supposed to tell from here if it had been a bird, a monkey, an innocent hiker . . . or the wedding saboteur?

Just then I felt my toe scrape against something. Luckily it was just a rock and not coral, but I decided I'd better pay more attention to what I was doing, especially since the water was now shallow enough for us to walk upright. I wasn't likely to see anything useful on shore anyway—anybody could be hiding anywhere in that jungle.

"Hey!" a shout came from the beach.

Looking up from picking my way among the coral formations, I saw that a small crowd had gathered there while we were swimming. Vic was at the front, standing calf-deep in the water, staring our way.

"We're okay, Vic!" Sydney called breathlessly, waving to him.

"Yeah," George added. "We—ow!"

I glanced over to see her dancing on one foot in the water, which was about waist-high by now. "You okay?"

"I'll live." She peered down at her foot. "I hope there are no sharks around here, though. I think I'm bleeding a little."

We pushed forward through the shallows. Vic rushed in to grab Sydney and sweep her into his arms. She hugged him around the neck.

"What happened, babe?" he asked, hugging her back and then gently pushing her bedraggled red hair out of her face with one hand. "Trouble with the boat?"

Someone had turned off the boom box by now. But I realized its loud music must have masked the sound of those shots.

"Not exactly," I said carefully, glancing toward the cameras. There were two cameramen there filming the scene from different angles, though I couldn't help noticing that Butch wasn't one of them. In fact, aside from the two camera operators and an older woman from the makeup team, nobody from the TV crew was in view at the moment.

"Wow, that looks painful," Bess was saying to George, bending over to peer at the cut on her foot. "You might want to get it looked at."

A uniformed resort employee pushed forward. "Yes, please come with me, miss," he said in a polite but firm voice. "I'll take you to the medical hut straightaway."

"Don't be silly," George protested. "It's just a little scrape. All I need is a Band-Aid."

But the employee wouldn't take no for an answer, explaining that coral cuts could be very dangerous if left untreated. George insisted it had been a sharp rock she'd stepped on rather than coral, but evidently the resort wanted to take no chances. Soon the young man and another employee were hustling her off down the beach.

Meanwhile I sidled toward another uniformed employee, an intelligent-looking middle-aged woman. "Listen," I whispered to her. "I don't want this to be on camera, but you should know—someone shot at us."

The woman blinked and turned to stare at me. "I beg your pardon?"

I repeated the information, adding that I was pretty sure the shots had come from the direction of the jungle. By the time I finished, the employee was already shaking her head.

"I'm sure this was a very frightening experience, miss," she said in a smooth, sympathetic voice. "But as the person who gave you that boat should have explained, there are a few spots with very sharp coral that can tear the rubber pontoons if one isn't careful. I'm sorry you weren't properly warned about this."

"No, you don't understand." I cast another quick look around to make sure neither of the cameras was too close. "It wasn't the coral. Someone shot out those pontoons! You'll see when you bring the boat in."

"All right, we'll take that under advisement." The woman's tone indicated quite plainly that she was humoring me, though her polite smile never wavered. "I'll send someone out to get it first thing tomorrow."

"Tomorrow?" I exclaimed. "No, you need to bring it in now! If someone looks at the punctures, maybe . . ."

My voice trailed off as I realized one of the cameramen had stepped closer and was filming me. The other camera was still aimed at Sydney and Vic.

"I'm very sorry your visit with us started out with this sort of unfortunate occurrence," the employee said in that same smooth, professional voice. "We at the Oro Beach Resort would like to make it up to you with a complimentary massage at our world-class spa."

With that, she turned away. I stared at the back of her head, feeling frustrated. Chief McGinnis of the River Heights Police Department might not be the sharpest tack on the bulletin board, but at least he usually took me seriously! It was clear this woman didn't. She wasn't even planning to drag that pontoon boat out of the lagoon until the next day, let alone warn people that there might be a gun-toting maniac on the loose. So what was I supposed to do now?

I glanced around. Vic was still holding Sydney. She was crying, and he was trying to shield her from the camera with his body. Nearby, Bo and Jamal were just standing there, shifting their weight from foot to foot and looking uncertain.

"Please!" Sydney wailed as the cameraman stepped around for a better angle. "Can't you just leave us alone for a second?"

Vic glared at the cameraman. "Yeah, have a heart, dude," he said. "Give us a sec, okay?"

"Sorry, Vic. Just doing my job," the cameraman responded calmly, taking a step closer and focusing on Sydney.

Vic scowled and gently lowered his new wife to the sand. "Listen," he blustered, clenching his fists. "You know I'm usually cool with the whole all-access thing. But I asked you nicely, and now I'm telling you. Back off. Or I'll have to make you do it."

Uh-oh. He sounded pretty steamed. And it looked like the cameraman wasn't planning to back down—

he was a big guy, almost as broad and burly as Butch or Bo. I glanced around, wishing Madge or Donald was around to break this up, but neither of them was anywhere in sight.

"Listen, both of you," Bess said in her most soothing tone. "Let's just take a deep breath. . . ."

"Yes, please," added the female employee I'd spoken to. "I'm sure we can work things out, gentlemen."

Vic just glared at her. Before he could respond, there was a loud buzz from the direction of some beach chairs nearby.

"Dude, it's your phone," Bo said, grabbing something off one of the chairs and tossing it to Vic.

Vic caught the cell phone and glanced at it, seeming distracted. Then he blinked and brought the phone closer to his face, peering at the tiny screen with an expression of confusion and dismay.

"What is it, Vic?" Sydney asked, stepping closer for a look. When she saw whatever was on the phone, she let out a loud gasp. "Oh, no!" she cried.

"Hey!" Madge's loud, abrasive voice broke into the scene. She came barreling onto the beach. "What's going on? Heard there was some kind of trouble."

"What is it, man?" Jamal asked, staring at Vic with concern.

Vic glanced at him, then over at Bo. "Nothing," he said. "It's nothing. Just that guy we met in Seattle."

Bo nodded. Then he glanced out toward the lagoon. His eyes widened, and he jumped forward, pointing out that way.

"Hey, check it out!" he shouted. "Shark!"

FINNY BUSINESS

Bo's sudden outburst caused another flurry of exclamations and shouts of alarm. "Are you serious? There's a shark out there?" Madge cried. She turned and jabbed a finger at the cameramen. "This is golden. Get it on film!"

Both cameramen were way ahead of her. Their lenses were already turned out toward the waters of the lagoon, searching for the shark.

"Hang on, I'm on it!" Bo hollered, ripping off his T-shirt. "Yo, I've always wanted to wrestle a shark. *Banzai!*"

He raced down toward the water's edge and flung himself in, causing a huge splash. I just stared along with everyone else, startled and a little confused by this turn of events.

"Where is it?" Bess stepped over next to me, shading her eyes with one hand. "I don't see any shark."

"Me either." I was already starting to recover from my surprise.

Madge was standing at the water's edge, not seeming to notice that tiny, gentle waves were lapping over the toes of her expensive-looking leather pumps. One of the cameramen was in up to his knees, while the other had scooted down the beach to catch another angle.

Bo was a pretty strong swimmer and was already a good distance out. He stopped and came up for air.

"There it is!" he yelled, waving one hand vaguely ahead of him. Then he let out an excited whoop. "Yeah, you *better* swim away from me, Jaws, if you know what's good for you!"

He flung himself forward again, swimming hard. "Whoa," Madge muttered. She shot a look at the cameramen. "This could be huge! Keep on him, guys."

"You go, Bo!" Jamal shouted, dancing around at the edge of the water pumping both fists in the air. "You'll show that shark who's boss, boy!"

I was surprised anew by that. It was never a surprise to see Bo or Vic hamming it up for the cameras. But Jamal hadn't really seemed like the type.

I glanced over to see how Sydney was taking all this. She was already on edge, and I was afraid a random shark appearance might be all that was needed to send her over it.

But to my further surprise, she was nowhere in sight. Neither was Vic. The two of them had disappeared during all the commotion!

Just then Bess nudged me. "Come on," she whispered. "This way."

Feeling a little confused, I followed as she tiptoed away, staying out of Madge's sight line. We both ducked behind a neatly clipped hedge at the edge of the beach and hurried along until we were well hidden behind an equipment shed. We rounded the corner and saw Sydney and Vic there waiting for us.

Now I realized what was happening. "You mean the shark thing is a ruse?" I asked Vic, feeling slightly sheepish for taking so long to catch on.

He shrugged. "It's a code Bo and I invented," he explained, glancing out around the edge of the shed to check that Bess and I hadn't been followed. "We use it back in NYC all the time. Whenever one of us mentions a guy from Seattle, the other one's supposed to kick up a scene as a distraction."

"Oh." I glanced at Bess, realizing there was one

mystery remaining about all this. "But wait, how did you know where they went?"

"As soon as we got out of the way, we tried to text you, Nancy," Sydney spoke up. "But I guess your phone's not working or something, because you didn't answer."

I touched the pocket of my shorts. "Oh. I guess I forgot to get it out of my bag after we left the airport. Just as well, since it would've gotten soaked when we ended up in the lagoon."

"Luckily mine's got a water-resistant case," Bess said. "They tried me next."

I nodded, glancing at the couple. Vic looked grim and pale, and Sydney had stopped crying but still appeared to be pretty worked up.

"Okay," I said briskly. "So does this mean we finally get to talk about that mess you guys found in your room when you got here? Or did you guys have any ideas about what happened with the pontoon boat?"

"Sure, we can talk about that stuff if you want. But first . . ." Vic pulled out his cell phone and held it out to me. "This just came."

Once again, I felt a little slow as I remembered that a message had come in for him right before the shark thing—a message that had made Sydney gasp in alarm and get even more upset than she'd already been.

"Oh, right," I said, reaching for the phone. "What's it say?"

Glancing down, I saw an e-mail blinking on the screen. The text consisted of a single line: TELL YOUR BRIDE SHE CAN'T ESCAPE FROM HER SHADOW.

But that wasn't all. Below that message was a photo. It showed the lagoon right there at the resort under the moonlight—with the back view of a shiny bald head sticking up from the dark water!

"Whoa," I murmured, realizing what this meant.

MrSilhouette was back. And he was right here at the resort.

SAFE HOUSE

"It's from MrSilhouette!" Sydney cried, sounding on the verge of hysteria. "I should have known it wasn't over. He's here! He has to be the one doing all this terrible stuff. What am I going to do?" She turned and buried her face in Vic's chest. "I never should have agreed to marry you," she sobbed, her words slightly muffled. "Now you're in danger too."

"It's okay, love," he said, rubbing her head soothingly. "We'll get through this."

Bess stepped over and patted Sydney on the back. "Yeah, try not to let it get to you so much, Syd," she added. "Nancy's on the case now—she'll track this guy down. She always gets her man."

I barely heard her. This was an alarming new development. Of course I'd known all along that there was a pretty good chance that Sydney's old stalker could be behind all the trouble. But this appeared to prove it. I stared at the message and photo, wishing George was there to try to track who'd sent it.

Never mind, I told myself, realizing it probably wouldn't do any good. This guy was a pro—even the NYPD hadn't been able to trace his first batch of e-mails. Somehow I doubted he'd gotten any sloppier since then.

Still, I punched a few buttons to forward the message to George's phone, hoping it hadn't been totally ruined by its saltwater bath. Just as I finished, the phone buzzed in my hand.

"Incoming message," I said.

"Got it," Vic said, grabbing the phone out of my hand before I could see who the message was from. He glanced at the screen, then immediately stuck the phone in his pocket. "Just my agent," he said with a shrug. "I'll call him back later."

He sounded kind of jumpy. And no wonder. We were all a little jumpy at this point.

Sydney was still sobbing inconsolably against Vic's chest, with Bess crooning into her ear to no apparent avail. Vic glanced around, still looking nervous.

"I think I'd better take her somewhere more

private to get her settled down," he said. "When Madge and the others notice we're gone . . ."

I nodded. The last thing Sydney needed right now was a camera shoved in her face. "How about our bungalow?" I suggested. "The TV people never bother to film the three of us unless we're with one of you guys, so you should be safe there for a while."

Bess cleared her throat. "Right," she said. "Except we don't really know where it is. I mean, we can follow the little map on the key, but we haven't been there ourselves yet, and so—"

"Never mind," Vic broke in. "Akinyi's hut is the first one out on the walk, right out there over the sand—she made them give her that one because she said she'd get seasick trying to sleep out over the water."

Despite the serious circumstances, I couldn't help a brief smile. Yeah, that sounded like Akinyi.

"She wasn't out there on the beach," I remembered. "So maybe she's in the bungalow."

Or maybe not, I realized with a flash of concern. After all, I'd originally suspected Akinyi and Jamal of causing all the trouble. Now that Pandora appeared to be innocent, did I need to consider whether I might have been right about the other two after all?

There was no time to think about that at the moment. We scooted out from our hiding place, tiptoeing across the beach toward the steps leading up to the warren of wooden walkways that stretched out over the water. Soon we were huddled on the tiny front porch of the first bungalow, with Bess keeping a lookout for roving cameramen while Vic knocked softly on the door. I stood behind him, one arm around Sydney, who leaned limply against me. In the distance we could still hear shouts and whoops, presumably from the Great Shark Hunt out in the lagoon.

"Who is it?" Akinyi's accented voice called out from inside.

"It's us! Let us in, okay?" Vic hissed, shooting a nervous look around at the nearby bungalows. We were hidden from the beach here, but not very well. Anyone could come down one of the walkways at any moment and spot us there.

Several long seconds passed before the door opened a crack. Akinyi peered out at us, looking wary. "Oh. It *is* you," she said, raising one perfectly groomed eyebrow when she took in the sight of Bess and me in our damp street clothes. "What is it? I just stepped out of the shower."

"Please let us in, Kinnie, okay?" Vic urged. "We just got some pretty wild news, and now Syd's upset, and we're trying to stay out of camera range. . . ."

"Oh, I see." Akinyi finally seemed to notice Sydney

standing there, and her face softened. "Just wait one second while I throw something on, all right?"

"Kinnie, wait!" Vic began. But it was too late. The door slammed in our faces.

"She'd better hurry up," Bess whispered from her vantage point at the edge of the porch. "It sounds like the fun's over out there."

Sure enough, the shouts had finally died down. I guessed there was only so long that Bo could pretend he was chasing a shark before it became obvious he wasn't actually going to catch anything.

"She should know she doesn't have to get all dressed up for us," I muttered, casting a look at Akinyi's door as several thumping noises came from inside. "What's taking her so long?"

Finally, after another few endless moments, the door opened again. This time Akinyi let it swing wide, revealing that she was wrapped in a plush terrycloth robe with the resort's logo printed on it.

Weird, I thought as we all rushed in. If she wasn't getting dressed, what was all the thumping about?

"Finally!" Vic blurted out. "I thought you'd never—whoa!"

He caught himself just in time as he stumbled and almost went flying. Glancing down, I saw that he'd tripped over a pair of muddy sandals that had been sitting just inside the door.

Akinyi glanced at them too. "Oh, sorry about that," she said, kicking the sandals out of the way under a nearby dresser. "I went for a walk in the rain forest to get away from the cameras for a while. That's why I was in the shower, actually." She shrugged. "It's a bit muddy out there."

Vic didn't seem too interested in any of that. "Listen, can we hide out here for a while?" he asked, already guiding Sydney toward the nearest chair. "It's been kind of a tough afternoon. See, first Sydney was out on the water with the girls when someone took a shot at them. . . ."

He went on to explain what had happened, from the pontoon incident to the message from MrSilhouette. Akinyi seemed alarmed by the former and positively horrified by the latter.

"No!" she blurted out, covering her mouth as Vic showed her the photo on his phone. "But I thought all that was over. Oh, Syd, this is terrible! You poor baby!" She rushed over and wrapped her long, slim arms around her friend.

"Come on," I murmured to Bess. "Let's leave them to it. We should go get George and then find our bungalow." A lot had happened since we'd arrived on the island just a couple of hours earlier, and my head was spinning. It was way past time to sit down, catch my breath, huddle with my friends, and discuss it all privately.

★ ★ ★

An hour later my friends and I were sitting on the deck of our swank private bungalow. It consisted of a small but luxurious sitting room flanked by two bedrooms, one with a double bed and the other with two singles. George had immediately claimed the private room on the basis that she was injured and needed her rest.

"Oh, please." Bess had let out a snort. "It looks like they just stuck on a Band-Aid, like you wanted in the first place."

George had merely smirked and kicked her duffel bag away from the pile of luggage the resort staff had left in the center of the main room, aiming it in the direction of the bedroom door. "You should be nicer to me, cousin dearest. Coral cuts can be deadly, you know. In fact, the guys at the med hut were telling me there's all kinds of ways to get injured or killed around this part of the Caribbean. Coral, sharks, snakes, jellyfish, scorpions, puffer fish, lionfish, eels, even some kind of weird dangerous algae . . ."

I managed to get them back on track, and we quickly stowed our stuff in our respective rooms, changed into dry clothes, and then went out to the bungalow's small front porch to discuss things. There were three deck chairs out there that offered a great view of the lagoon. They also offered a pretty close-up view of the bungalows on either side of ours. Only about ten yards of water separated each of their porches from ours.

"Are you sure it's safe to talk out here?" Bess asked, casting an anxious glance at one of the neighboring bungalows.

George shrugged and followed her gaze. "They're not that close. We'll just keep our voices down. Besides, it doesn't look like anybody's home."

"I hope not." Bess still looked worried. "Sound carries over water, remember."

"Well, it's not like we'll be much safer inside," I pointed out. "The hut's walls seem pretty thin." I shrugged. "Anyway, George is probably right. The show rented out this entire resort, remember? The crew is probably all out doing their thing, and we know where Syd and Vic and their friends are."

"I guess you're right." Bess glanced at me. "So what do you think of the case so far, Nancy? Do you really think MrSilhouette is on the loose here somewhere?"

"It sure seems like it, doesn't it?" I rubbed my chin thoughtfully, gazing down at the tiny waves lapping against the pilings of the walkway. "But we shouldn't rule out other possibilities, either. Candy faked that 'gift' from MrSilhouette before, remember?"

"You mean you think someone might've faked

that photo of him too?" George said. "But who?"

"I don't know," I said. "Any of our list of suspects could be behind it, I guess. There's Butch, for one. . . ."

"Unless he's MrSilhouette himself," Bess put in.

I nodded. "Right. But anyway, that photo isn't that clear. What if someone brought one of those fake bald head cover thingies like they use on TV? Or even snagged one of the mannequins from the shops here at the resort—I'm pretty sure most of those probably have bald heads so the window dressers can put different wigs on them when they change out the displays."

"Good point." Bess looked impressed and thoughtful. "But I still can't figure out who would want to make Syd's life miserable like this. Other than her stalker, I mean—I get that motive. He wouldn't want her to be happy with anyone other than him."

"Well, what about Akinyi and Jamal?" I kicked at a knot in the porch floor. "We thought they were cleared when Pandora pulled that knife, but . . ."

Bess gasped. "Oh, wow! I hadn't even thought of that!" she exclaimed. "You mean you think they might have been behind the trouble after all?"

"Not necessarily." I bit my lip, remembering with some discomfort how upset and disappointed the pair had been about missing the wedding, and their touching reunion with Sydney and Vic at the reception after being released by the police. "But we don't want to rule anything out, either."

"Hang on—but Jamal couldn't have been the one who shot at us," George pointed out. "He was on the beach with Vic the whole time, remember?"

"Oh!" Bess's eyes widened. "But Akinyi was nowhere in sight. And there was mud all over her cute Louboutins, remember?"

"Her what?" George blinked in confusion.

"The sandals," I said grimly. "She even said she'd been for a walk in the jungle. And she definitely didn't want to let us in when we first got there—almost like she needed time to hide something first."

"Something like a gun?" Now George looked alarmed. "Whoa."

"And she and Jamal arrived on the island earlier than everyone else," I reminded my friends. "So that would've given them plenty of time if they were the ones who ransacked Syd and Vic's cabin. . . ."

"Oh! That reminds me." George sat up straight. "While I was at the med hut, I was chatting with the guys there like I said—"

"Right," Bess broke in dryly. "The Wild Wilds of Dangerous Nature gang."

George ignored her. "—and they told me which bungalow it was. The one that got ransacked, I mean. Apparently there are three honeymoon huts here, and after what happened, the resort moved Syd and Vic to a brand-new one right away."

"Really?" Now I was the one who sat bolt upright. "Did they say if the vandalized one had been cleaned up yet?"

"They said it was, just as soon as the local police finished up there yesterday," George said. "But you never know. . . ."

I was already jumping to my feet. "Do you think you can find it?"

"Definitely." George stood up too, as did Bess. "Come on, let's go take a look."

Soon we were creeping cautiously along the wooden walkways once more. It wasn't easy to stay inconspicuous. As I said, the walkways crisscross over the shallows of the lagoon, leading in a sort of meandering maze from one bungalow to another. In between, they're pretty much open to full view from every direction. Still, we did our best to hurry along those sections and keep a lookout for anyone who might be glancing our way.

Finally we reached the bungalow in question. It was made of palm thatch and bamboo like all the rest, but was larger and fancier, with a silky two-person hammock strung on the flower-draped porch.

"Think you can pick the lock?" I whispered to Bess.

She nodded with confidence. Bess might look like a helpless girly-girl on the outside, but she's anything but. She's got a natural talent for fixing things, from cars to toasters and everything in between. Picking a lock is usually a piece of cake for her.

"See anyone?" she muttered, sidling toward the front door. "It might take me a minute here, since they use those computerized key cards. . . ."

She reached for the door, automatically testing the knob. To all of our surprise, the door immediately swung open.

"Wow," George said with a slight smirk. "You're even better than I thought."

"Come on," I murmured, already darting through the door.

The window shades were all down, making the interior of the honeymoon bungalow dim and shadowy. Even so, it was immediately obvious that the place had already been straightened up just as the employees had told George.

"Looks like they did a good job," George said, glancing around the spotless sitting room. "Figures. A place like this doesn't mess around."

Bess had wandered farther into the room. "As long as we're here, I want to see what the honeymoon suite is— Hey! What's that?"

Taking note of the curious tone in her voice, I

hurried over to join her in the bedroom doorway. The bedroom was just as luxurious and spotless as the outer room. The only thing that seemed out of place was a sheet of paper lying on the bedspread.

George was peering over our shoulders by now. "What's the big deal?" she said. "Probably just a welcome note for the next set of honeymooners."

"Maybe." But I doubted it. My heart was thumping. I have a sort of sixth sense about things sometimes—George likes to call it my hunch-o-meter. And it was going off now.

I walked over and pushed aside the mosquito netting surrounding the bed. My eyes widened as soon as I got a clearer look at the paper.

"It's not a welcome note," I said grimly, picking it up. "At least not the kind you meant."

It was an ordinary sheet of white paper. Someone had used a black marker to draw a bulbous shape that took up more than half the sheet. Written below the drawing in a rough scrawl were the words: Mrs SEES & HEARS ALL.

"Whoa!" George let out a low whistle as she took a look. "MrSilhouette strikes again!"

"Looks that way." I stared at the paper.

Bess looked alarmed. "Is that drawing supposed to be his bald head?"

"Must be," George said. "But why'd he leave the

message here? Syd and Vic aren't even coming back to this room."

"Maybe he doesn't know that," I suggested. "In which case, maybe he doesn't see and hear quite as much as he thinks."

"But if he's here at the resort, wouldn't he have to know they're in another cabin?" Bess pointed out. "Especially if he's disguised as, like, a member of the crew or if it's Akinyi and Jamal. . . ."

"Good question." I frowned down at the paper, trying to puzzle out exactly what this meant. "Could he be hiding somewhere else on the island? Or maybe even doing things remotely from back in the U.S., maybe paying off locals to wreck the room and do the other stuff, or—"

Bess was nodding with interest, but George had turned away, not seeming to be paying attention. "Hey," she broke in, sniffing at the air. "Does anyone else smell smoke?"

I hadn't until that moment. But now that she mentioned it, I did. "Is that coming from outside?" I asked.

Bess reached the bedroom doorway in two strides. Peering out into the main room, she gasped. "No!" she cried. "This place is on fire!"

BURNING QUESTIONS

George and I raced over and saw that she was right. Fingers of flame were licking at the fabric shades on a couple of the windows, and the sofa and one of the wicker chairs were already fully engulfed. "Hurry!" I yelled, coughing from the thickening smoke. "Let's get out of here!"

Bess led the way to the door. It was closed. When she yanked on it, it didn't budge.

"It's locked!" she cried.

"It can't be. Let me try." George pushed past her and grabbed the knob, pushing and pulling at it desperately. "No way! Now what?"

I was already scanning around. The fire was growing with every passing second—we didn't have much time to find a way out. As soon as the flames reached the dry thatched roof, the whole place would become a deadly fireball.

"Check the windows!" I choked out, doing my best to cover my nose and mouth with the neck of my T-shirt.

I ran over to the closest one that wasn't aflame. Scrabbling past the shade, I found a metal screen attached firmly to the sturdy wooden frame. My first attempt to punch through it left me with nothing but scraped knuckles to show for it. Holding my breath, I leaned forward to try to see if there was an easy way to unlatch it. My heart sank as I saw that it appeared to be bolted firmly in place with several large screws.

"Over here!" Bess called.

I turned and squinted through the hazy smoke inside the cabin. She was just tucking something into the pocket of her shorts. A second later, coughing nonstop, she hoisted herself onto the windowsill and kicked out the screen.

George and I raced over. "Go! Go!" George shouted.

Bess didn't need to be told twice. She flung herself out through the window, and a second later I heard a splash from somewhere below. George was already climbing over the sill, and as soon as she jumped, it was my turn.

I swung my leg out the window and glanced around. The walkway outside the bungalow was already on fire, and I heard the faint sounds of shouts from somewhere off in the distance, telling me that someone had noticed the smoke. But there was no time to think about that—I could feel the heat on my back as I glanced down at the lagoon below. My friends had already moved aside, wading through the chest-high water toward shore.

"Seems like I'm spending an awful lot of time in this darn lagoon, considering I haven't even had a chance to unpack my bathing suit yet," I muttered. Then, taking a deep breath, I launched myself through the window.

"Butch!" Madge howled. "What are you doing? Get closer! We're going to want as much footage as we can get of this!" She stabbed one manicured finger toward someone. "You!" she barked. "Get those three looking camera-ready. What are you waiting for?"

I closed my eyes as Lainie, the makeup girl, hurried over, makeup brush in hand. My head was spinning after all that had happened; I hadn't had a moment to process things since splashing down in the lagoon. Thanks to Bess and the tiny multi-tool on the key ring hanging from her wallet, we'd escaped through that window just in the nick of time. Even as the three of us were wading toward the small crowd waiting for us on the beach, the roof had gone up with a loud *WHOOOMP*, raining sparks over us.

Now, nearly half an hour later, the fire was out—thanks to its position over the lagoon, the employees had been able to get things under control well before the local fire brigade had arrived to finish the job. The firefighters were currently stomping around through the shallow water checking for stray sparks or whatever, while most of the staff of the resort was gathered on the beach nearby watching. The honeymoon bungalow was nothing but a pile of ashes, and several sections of the walkway nearby had been destroyed as well. But the fire hadn't spread to any of the other structures, and for that, the resort manager appeared to be grateful.

However, one person was acting anything but grateful. Madge seemed to take it as a personal affront that the cameras hadn't been there to capture the dramatic moment when the bungalow had gone up in flames. She was making up for it now, ordering the entire camera team around without seeming to pause for breath.

"Chill, dude," Bo told the assistant director as she started haranguing one of the sound people for something or other. "You already missed the fun stuff. So what's the hurry?"

I cracked one eye open just in time to see Madge glare at him. "Do you want to take over?" she snapped. "Because my job's not as easy as you all seem to think."

Bo rolled his eyes and glanced over at Jamal and Akinyi, who had also turned up to watch. They both shrugged, seeming disinclined to get involved.

I kept my one open eye trained on the couple. How quickly had they turned up at the scene of the fire? I wasn't sure, but I knew they'd arrived before Madge and the crew. Did that mean something? I wasn't sure.

"Wait, what are you doing?" I opened my other eye as I felt Lainie begin to apply something thick and dusty to my forehead.

"Sorry. Madge's orders." Lainie held up a makeup brush with black powder flaking off it. "She wants to make sure you guys look really dramatic, so she ordered me to add some sooty smudges to your face." Shooting a slightly nervous look over her shoulder, she added, "And it's never a good idea to ignore Madge's orders, if you know what I mean."

"Maybe you're scared of her, but I'm not." Brushing aside the makeup brush, I took a step toward Madge. "Look, I think that's enough of the filming, okay?" I said loudly, putting up my hand to block the lens of the closest camera. "My friends and I just want to get back to our bungalow and clean ourselves up."

"Nancy's right," George agreed, shooing away another makeup artist. "We're out of here."

"What are you talking about?" Madge scowled at both of us. "You signed the releases. And this is a reality show—we're just filming what happened."

"Oh, really?" Bess spoke up. "So it's reality when you want me to rip a sleeve off my favorite shirt just because you say it'll make good TV?"

Madge just sputtered for a moment, looking even more irate than usual. "Cut!" she spat out at last, spinning toward the cameras and making a choppy slashing movement across her own throat with one thin hand. "Turn them off!"

"That's more like—" I began, ready to appease her a bit if necessary.

Before I could finish, she spun back around to face me and my friends, her eyes all but shooting sparks. "That's enough!" she hissed. "I should have known you three were only here to cause trouble. What's your angle? Let me guess—you're actually plants from *Winners and Losers*, right?"

"Huh?" I goggled at her, taken aback.

"*Winners and Losers* is another reality show,"

George said with a frown. "It's *Daredevils*'s biggest ratings rival, actually."

"That's right." Madge crossed her arms over her chest and glared. "And if you think you're going to sabotage this production, you've got another thing coming! I had enough of that back on the mainland, and now that I'm in charge, I'm going to make sure you don't cause any more trouble, do you hear me?"

Wait—so Madge thought *we* were the saboteurs? I was so stunned I could barely react.

"Madge!" Donald rushed up at that moment, breathless and red-faced. "There you are!" He stopped short, taking in the sight of the burned bungalow. "Hey, what happened?"

"What do *you* want?" Madge snapped, rounding on him with a glare. "Can't you see I'm busy here?"

Donald took a half step backward. "S-sorry," he stammered. "You told me to let you know if Vic or Sydney turned up, and I wanted to let you know I just spotted Vic heading toward the snack bar."

Madge was silent for a second, glowering at him, then at us. Finally she shrugged. "Fine," she snapped out. "Come on, guys. Let's go film Vic eating his cheeseburger or whatever. Might be boring, but I'm not about to give *Winners and Losers* any more free publicity for their sick little game."

With one last snarl in our general direction, she

stalked off. The camera operators exchanged glances and shrugs, then followed. Donald shot one last confused look at the charred remains of the honeymoon bungalow and trailed after them.

"Whew!" George breathed out, shaking her head slowly as she watched them all disappear. "That was . . . interesting."

"Yeah." I drifted a few steps in the direction Madge and Co. had gone, my mind churning. Could the assistant director really think my friends and I were the saboteurs? Or was this some kind of ruse, a distraction to keep us from suspecting *her*?

Before I could reach any conclusions, a bit of conversation drifted my way from nearby. Two young women wearing maids' uniforms were standing on the beach a few feet away, staring out at the scene of the fire. ". . . so it looks like we wasted our time getting Suite 1 fixed up so fast, didn't we?" one of the maids griped.

"Don't complain," the second employee said. "We got paid overtime for it, remember?"

I hurried toward them. "Excuse me," I said with a friendly smile. "So you two helped with the cleanup after the vandalism, huh? I guess you must have gotten a good look at that message someone wrote on the wall in there, right?"

The two employees went silent, trading a cautious

glance and then shrugging in unison. "We're sorry for this unpleasant moment in your Oro Beach Resort experience," the second maid said, sounding like some kind of recording. "We hope it won't mar your enjoyment of our beautiful island."

"Okay," I said. "But listen, I'd really like to know exactly what you guys saw before the cleanup. If you could just describe it in your own words . . ."

"I'm afraid we have to be getting back to work now," the employee said in that same robot-cruise-director voice. "If you have questions about your Oro Beach experience, feel free to visit our guest courtesy center in the main tiki hut."

"I don't want to visit the courtesy center," I said, doing my best not to sound as impatient as I felt. Out of the corner of my eye, I could see Bess and George trading amused glances. "I just want to hear what you two saw. If you're worried about marring my enjoyment or whatever, don't be. Sydney already showed me a picture of that ransacked cabin." I smiled hopefully. "Plus I won't tell your boss you said a word, I swear."

"It's not that." This time it was the first maid who spoke. She shot a look at her coworker, who looked worried. "I mean, yeah, the resort doesn't like us talking to the guests about stuff like that, I guess." She shrugged. "Not that we've ever had stuff like that happen before . . ."

"It's that director woman," the other maid burst out. "She made us sign something."

"You mean Madge?" George spoke up, sounding interested. "What, you mean like a film release?"

"Well, that, too." The first maid shrugged again. "But also this thing about not talking to people. Basically we're under orders not to say anything to anyone about anything that happens while filming is going on."

"Right." The second maid tugged at her friend's sleeve, shooting a nervous glance around the beach. "Now we really do have to get back to work. Excuse us, please."

They hurried off without a backward glance. "Wow," Bess said. "That's interesting, huh?"

"Not really." George fell into step beside me as I wandered down the beach after the maids. "It's probably standard operating procedure for this sort of production. A way to guarantee that spoilers don't leak out before the show airs, stuff like that. I'll have to ask my mom, but I'd be willing to guess that she had to sign something similar when she was catering some of those events before the wedding."

"That makes sense." Bess nodded. "Besides, Madge just accused the three of us of being behind all the trouble. That seems to let her off as a suspect herself, right?"

"Not necessarily," I said. "I'm really not sure what to make of Madge, actually. But guilty or not, one thing's for sure. She's definitely making our job harder. How are we supposed to investigate when the entire resort staff is under orders not to talk to anyone?"

"Maybe we should go talk to the people at the med hut again," George said as we climbed a few wooden steps leading from the beach up to the main section of the resort. "They were willing to talk. Although I kind of got the impression that they don't leave the med hut much. They kept complaining about it, actually—"

"Hey, do you hear that?" Bess broke in, casting a glance off to the right.

"Hear what?" But even as I said it, I heard the sound of shouts and shrieks from somewhere over that way.

George glanced at the rustic wooden signs that marked an intersection of paths just ahead. "Must be coming from the main pool," she said. "Should we go check it out? We haven't been over there yet."

"Yes we have," Bess said. "We passed it when we first got here, remember? Just before we saw Akinyi doing that modeling shoot."

George shook her head. "Didn't you read those brochures I printed off the Internet before we came?" she asked. "There are at least three pools here. That smallish one by the shops is called, like, the spa pool or something. Then there's the main pool over here, which is much bigger. And I'm pretty sure there's a lap pool over near the gym too."

While she was talking, we were hurrying along the path toward the main pool. We emerged from between two buildings to a panoramic view of it.

The pool was just what you'd expect to find in a tropical paradise. It was free-form and huge, with a couple of picturesque bridges leading over some narrow parts, a swim-up bar, several diving platforms, and at least three separate waterfall areas. The largest of the waterfalls tumbled down an impressive thirty-foot mountain of boulders that rose along the deep end of the largest section of the pool.

"Wow," Bess said. "This is nice!"

I nodded, glancing around the pool area. The yells appeared to have come from Vic, Bo, and Jamal, who were clowning around on the pavement at the base of the stone waterfall while Akinyi watched from a nearby lounge chair. All of the cameramen were there filming away from various angles. Madge, Donald, and Lainie, along with a few other assorted crew members, were looking on from just out of camera range.

None of them seemed to notice our arrival. As we watched, Vic danced over toward Akinyi. "Be a sport,

Kinnie!" he exclaimed with a wicked grin, advancing on her as she glanced up from the magazine she was reading. "Either come on in for a swim, or I'll have to make you come in!"

"Don't you dare!" Akinyi warned with a frown, holding up one long, slim finger and shaking it at him sternly. "I just did my hair. If you mess it up, I'll kill you!"

Vic pretended to cower away while Jamal snorted with amusement. Meanwhile Bo let out a shout of laughter. "Hey, if she won't take a dip with us, we'll just have to find another pretty girl who will! And look, there's one right over there!" He leaped toward Lainie. "How about it? Want to get wet, darlin'?"

Vic, Jamal, and even Akinyi were already chuckling. But Lainie immediately jumped back, avoiding Bo as he reached for her arm. "No!" she cried.

"Guess she's not supposed to let herself be seen on camera," Bess murmured.

George shrugged. "Doesn't look like the camera guys are following that rule," she observed. "See? They're shooting all this—well, except for that Butch guy—and Madge isn't complaining."

I saw that she was right. Butch seemed to be taking a break—he was over in the shade of a beach umbrella sipping a bottle of water and talking with Donald— but the other camera operators were all focused right in on Lainie and Bo. Madge was watching the whole scene with her usual hawklike intensity, not saying a word.

"Good point." I frowned slightly as I returned my attention to Lainie, whose protests were getting louder and more panicky-sounding with each new lunge out of Bo's grasp. "And actually, she looks pretty upset. For real, I mean, not just flirty-upset."

Bess nodded. "I think you're right."

"Well, you *are* the expert when it comes to flirting, cuz," George joked.

"Please!" Lainie cried loudly at that moment, once more wriggling free as Bo grabbed at her arm. "Leave me alone!" Whirling around, she raced around the edge of the pool and disappeared into a grove of palm trees, looking near tears.

"Lainie?" Bo called after her, sounding confused. Then he turned and shrugged at his friends. "Dude! What was that all about? I was just kidding around."

"Maybe she can't swim," Jamal suggested.

"Yeah. Or maybe she just didn't want you to touch her—couldn't blame her for that." Vic grinned as Bo pretended to take a swing at him. "Never mind, looks like it's just us guys. Last one in's a rotten egg!"

Letting out a whoop, he raced over and flung himself into the deep end, landing in a sloppy cannonball with a loud splash. Both of the other guys followed, hitting the water at the same time. Soon all three of them were bobbing around out there. Vic floated on his back, closing his eyes as he drifted under the edge of the waterfall.

Meanwhile Butch had finished his break and was now filming away with the others. "You're not giving us much here, guys," he called out in his usual gruff way. "How's about doing something we couldn't film at any kiddie pool in the world?"

"Like what?" Vic flipped over and started treading water. "You want me to ride a Jet Ski through here or something?"

Butch let out a snort. "Look, I'm just saying. We only have a week on this boring little island, and your girl seems to be in hiding, and Eberhart'll flip if we don't get anything he can use."

"Yeah, he's right about that," Madge muttered. "Where *is* that Sydney, anyway?"

"So what did you have in mind, bro?" Vic asked Butch loudly. I could tell he was deliberately ignoring the question about Sydney's whereabouts. "I mean, this is a pool, not a stunt show."

"Look, I dunno. I'm no director." Butch shot a look at the thirty-foot rock mountain. "You could climb up there and dive in or something. Even that'd be more *Daredevils* than floating around like a bunch of old ladies."

Vic cast a lazy glance up at the wall. Then he turned over on his back again, not rising to the cameraman's taunt.

"Maybe later," he said with a yawn. "It's been a long week, you know?"

Butch scowled. "Gonna be a lot of long weeks if you actually land the cohosting gig next season, boy," he muttered.

"Whatever." Vic yawned, then glanced over at Bo. "How about if Captain Champion here goes first? I dare you, dude."

Bo squinted up the mountain too. "I dunno," he said. "Looks like a tough climb, and I'm in relaxation mode right now, you know?"

Just then I caught a flash of movement at the edge of the palm grove. Glancing over, I saw that Lainie had just crept back into the pool area, looking slightly sheepish.

Bo spotted her too. "On the other hand, what the heck," he said, already swimming for the edge. "Anything to liven up this dead party, huh?"

He hoisted himself out of the pool, strutting and thumping his chest as he headed for the base of the man-made mountain. Soon he was clambering up, still shouting and showing off as usual.

"There you go," Vic told Butch. "Happy now?"

Butch just shrugged, turning his camera to follow

Bo. One of the other cameramen came over for a better angle too.

"Men!" Bess shook her head, looking amused. "They'll do anything to impress a pretty girl."

I chuckled. "Should we go check on Sydney?" I asked. "It seems like a good time to sneak over to Akinyi's cabin, with all the other major players occupied here."

"Sure." George shaded her eyes as she followed Bo's climb. "But wait, let's watch Bo jump first. I want to see if he lands on Vic or Jamal on his way down. That would be totally *Daredevils*."

Bo reached the top and raised both arms over his head. "I'm king of the world, baby!" he howled playfully, striding out toward a slab of stone overhanging the top of the waterfall. "I'm king of the— *oof!*"

The rock suddenly shifted with a sickening scraping sound. A second later it collapsed sideways, sending Bo tumbling head over heels, banging and crashing down the face of the rock wall.

SHADOWS, SACRIFICES, AND SUSPICIONS

"It's lucky Bo knows how to fall thanks to all his adventures on the show," George commented. It was dinnertime, and my friends and I had gathered in the open-air restaurant along with almost everyone else at the resort. All traces of Bo's earlier adventures with the fire juggling had been eradicated from view. But the same couldn't be said about his tumble from the top of the waterfall. His head was bandaged, one arm was in a sling, and he looked generally banged up and bruised.

Still, all things considered, he appeared to be in pretty good shape as I glanced over at the table where he was seated with Jamal and Akinyi. He was in his usual high spirits, letting out an occasional shout of laugher and trading high fives with Jamal with the arm that wasn't in a sling.

"You're right about that," I mused in response to George's remark, not taking my eyes off Bo. "If he hadn't managed to get himself right side up and push away from the wall when he got near the bottom . . ."

Bess shuddered. "Let's not talk about that," she said firmly, reaching for her water glass. "I'm just glad Sydney wasn't there to witness it."

"Where is Syd, anyway?" George glanced around the restaurant. "I haven't seen her since we dropped her off you-know-where, you-know-when."

I realized she was right. Sydney hadn't made an appearance since we'd left her in Akinyi's bungalow earlier.

"I don't know," I said. "But I really need to talk to her. Things are getting pretty serious—first the fire, which could have killed us, and now Bo's close call."

Just then I caught a commotion over near the entryway. Glancing over, I saw Vic and Sydney entering the dining area.

"There she is," I said.

Bess looked over too. "She looks pretty normal, considering."

That was true. Sydney was maybe a little paler

than usual, but otherwise looked as pretty and pulled together as ever. She clung to Vic's arm as the cameras swarmed around them.

"Hmm," I observed. "Looks like it could be a challenge to catch her alone."

"Maybe you can set up a meeting for later, like after the cameramen go to bed," George suggested.

"I really don't want to wait that long. Who knows how soon our culprit might strike again?"

"Good point." George shrugged. "For all we know, Vic's dinner might already be poisoned."

"Don't say that!" Bess looked alarmed.

I stood up as Sydney and Vic sat down with Akinyi, Bo, and Jamal. "Come on," I said. "There are still plenty of seats over at their table. Let's join them."

"Nancy! Girls!" Sydney looked up and smiled as we approached. "I was just about to call you over. I feel like I've barely had a chance to spend any time with you since you arrived." She shot me a meaningful look, but didn't say anything else.

"Yeah," I agreed, trying to sound casual and not look at any of the cameras that were filming us. "Maybe we can go for a walk on the beach after dinner or something."

"Sounds good," Butch muttered from behind his camera. "Madge wants more footage of the bride doing the island thing anyway."

I bit back a sigh. No, it wasn't going to be easy to get any time alone with Sydney. . . .

"So who's up for some Jet Ski action tomorrow?" Bo spoke up.

Akinyi stared at him. "You're planning to drive a Jet Ski with that sling on your arm?" she asked in clear disbelief.

"Oh, he won't let that stop him, trust me," Vic said with a chuckle. "One time on the show when we were doing a stunt at Mount Rushmore, the producers said he had to skip it because he'd sprained his wrist doing the last stunt, and . . ."

From there, they were off and running with a series of *Daredevils* stories. Under any other circumstances I probably would have found the tales and bragging amusing, and I was sure the audience of the TV special would eat them up. But at the moment all I could think about was finding an opportunity to talk privately with Sydney.

Finally it came. "Oh!" Akinyi shrieked, pushing back from the table so quickly that her chair almost tipped over backward. "Did you all see that? A fly! It was just—just walking across my food!"

"Oh, horrors!" Bo cried out in a falsetto, fanning himself dramatically with one hand. "A fly, you say?"

Akinyi glared at him. "Very funny," she snapped. "Just because you boys are happy to eat cow patties or whatever on your silly little show, it doesn't mean the rest of us care to poison ourselves."

"Cow patties?" Vic said. "We never ate cow patties. Now cow *eyeballs*, on the other hand . . ."

By then Akinyi's outburst had brought several resort employees running. They gathered around, a manager apologizing profusely as a waitress whisked away the tainted plate and the others busily shooed away every fly in the vicinity.

Taking advantage of the momentary hubbub, I leaned over to Sydney. "How about a run to the ladies' room?" I asked her.

She nodded and set down her napkin. "Right behind you."

As we stood up, Donald glanced over from the next table. "Where are you two going?" he called out.

"We'll be right back!" Sydney said cheerily. Then she grabbed my hand. "Hurry!" she hissed in my ear. "Before the cameras catch on!"

We scooted for the exit. Miraculously, we managed to escape the dining room before Donald could alert the cameramen. Once inside the nearest ladies' lounge, which was large and luxurious, Sydney collapsed into a chair in front of a wall of mirrors.

"Oh, Nancy," she said, her voice quavering. "I'm trying so hard to stay strong here. But with everything that's happened . . ."

I nodded sympathetically. As upset as she seemed, I was hesitant to tell her about that note we'd seen just before the fire. But she had to know what was going on.

"Listen, Syd." I took a deep breath. "There's something you need to hear about. . . ."

As I told her the whole story, her eyes widened more and more. "Oh, no!" she burst out when I'd finished. "I'm so sorry, Nancy. I'm sure that message was meant for me, and you and the girls almost got hurt instead!"

"I'm not so sure about that, actually. What if this MrSilhouette, whoever he really is, knows that I'm here to investigate the trouble?" I briefly flashed through the list of possible suspects. As far as I knew, only Vic and Akinyi knew I hadn't just gotten lucky busting Candy and later Pandora—that I was actually a pretty accomplished amateur sleuth. But that didn't mean any of the others couldn't have found out somehow. They'd all spent enough time in River Heights to have figured it out, since my rep is hardly a secret there.

Sydney was shaking her head, tears welling in her eyes. "Either way, it's all because of me," she moaned. "What if that nut sets another fire while Vic and I are sleeping?" Her hands flew to her face as another thought occurred to her. "Oh, and what if that had been Vic climbing the rocks over the pool today? He could have been killed!"

It almost *had* been Vic, I realized. That was who Butch had been goading into trying the stunt. . . .

Before I could explore that idea, though, I had to get Sydney calmed down. "Listen, it's up to you to decide what to do next," I told her. "I talked to the resort manager just before dinner, and she said that slab of rock over the pool was definitely loose, and that it shouldn't have been. But she seems to think it was an accident—something that happened while they were power washing the pool area or something."

"What about the fire?" Sydney asked. "They can't think that was an accident, can they? Especially with that horrible note you found!"

"Well, they are kind of disturbed that the smoke alarm never went off, but I didn't exactly tell anyone about the note yet," I admitted. "Mostly because I forgot in all the drama afterward. And then, well, considering the circumstances, I thought I'd better check in with you first about what to do next."

Sydney looked surprised. She was silent for a moment, staring at her own reflection in the mirror. I was half expecting her to say that she was going to leave the island, or at least that she wanted to call in the local authorities right away.

"I don't think you should tell anyone yet," she said at last. "I mean, I already went the police route the first time around, back in New York. Both the NYPD and that private investigator I hired tried and failed to track down MrSilhouette's identity before." She turned to face me. "So at this point, Nancy, I'm thinking you're my only hope."

What was I supposed to say to that? "Okay," I replied. "You know I'll do my best, Sydney. But this guy's tricky, so it might not be a bad idea to bring in reinforcements, or—"

"No," she broke in grimly. "Like I said, you're my only hope—or should I say my *last* hope. If you can't track down this crazy MrSilhouette guy in this place, this little resort on an island with hardly anyone around, then I'll just have to accept that it's hopeless. That I really will be looking over my shoulder, trying to catch a glimpse of that extra shadow behind me, for the rest of my life." She turned to stare at herself in the mirror again, her expression somber. "I've been thinking a lot about that possibility today, actually, and I've reached a decision. If we don't solve this thing before we all leave the island, I'm planning to leave Vic as soon as we get back to New York."

"What?" I squawked.

She nodded. "MrSilhouette obviously doesn't want to see me with anyone else. It seems like he's willing to do anything to make sure of it. I love Vic way too much to put him in that kind of danger."

"Sydney, think about what you're saying!" I exclaimed, horrified. "Vic loves you, too. And he's used to doing dangerous stuff—just talk to him first, okay?"

"I can't. You're right, he'll think he can handle it." Her lower lip quivered. "But how am I supposed to handle it when MrSilhouette finally succeeds one day and the love of my life ends up dead—because of me?"

I wasn't sure what to say to that. It was pretty obvious that Sydney's mind was made up. That meant I really was the only hope for her and Vic's future happiness. Talk about pressure!

Sure, I knew I could go to the authorities myself with what I'd seen in that honeymoon cabin. But without Sydney backing me up, would they believe me? Would they take action? I had to wonder, based on the resort employee's reaction when I'd told her about the pontoon shooting.

Besides that, if a bunch of cops swarmed into the resort, what was to stop MrSilhouette from going back into hiding? That might fix things for the short term, but Sydney would know he wasn't gone for good. That would almost guarantee that she'd follow through on her plans to leave Vic.

She turned away from the mirror to face me. "So?" she said. "How about it, Nancy? Will you help me?"

I took a deep breath, meeting her eye. "I'll do my best."

"I can't believe Syd's really planning to leave Vic for his own safety." Bess looked up from tucking some clothes into a drawer in our bungalow bedroom. "If it wasn't so serious, I'd say that was totally romantic!"

"Are you nuts?" George said, wandering into the room. "Syd and Vic are perfect for each other. We have to make sure it doesn't come to that."

I was perched on the edge of my bed watching Bess unpack. It was late, but I was feeling far too antsy to sleep—or even unpack my own suitcase beyond pulling out a nightgown and my toothbrush.

"So let's go over the case," I suggested. "Starting with Bo's fall. I can't help remembering that the whole climbing-the-waterfall thing was Butch's idea."

Bess's eyes widened. "You're right! And he actually wanted Vic to be the one to climb up there."

"Butch," George said. "*Bald* Butch. It all fits perfectly!"

I nodded thoughtfully. "Almost *too* perfectly. If

Butch is MrSilhouette, it would mean he's getting sloppy. He urged Vic to climb up there multiple times, right in front of a whole bunch of people—Bo, Jamal, Akinyi, us, Madge, Donald, the other cameramen . . . If the worst happened, that would've looked awfully suspicious."

"So what?" George argued. "If his plan had worked, and Vic had cracked his head open and died, everybody would've been too upset to think about that kind of thing. The resort probably would have accepted responsibility, and that would be that."

"Plus MrSilhouette would've had what he wanted—Sydney all to himself again," Bess pointed out. "He probably wouldn't even care if he got caught at that point."

My heart thumped. Could they be right? "So if what we're saying is true, that would mean that Butch—aka MrSilhouette—might have been right there under our noses the whole time," I said. "But could he have pulled off all the other unsolved mischief?"

"Well, he was certainly around for the jet fuel thing," George said. "And he might have sent those threatening texts and e-mails as easily as anyone."

Bess started ticking things off on her fingers. "He

probably could have been the one who ripped up Syd's wedding dress, and he definitely could've rigged that light that almost fell on Vic, and framed Pandora. . . ."

"Come on." I stood up and checked my watch. "It's after hours for the crew by now. Let's see if we can find where Butch is staying and maybe spy on him a little. If he is our bad guy, he might be plotting his next stunt right this very second."

It didn't take long for us to find Butch. That's because he was on the beach along with the rest of the crew. They were all having some kind of private party out there on the sand, whooping it up and having a great time. Even Madge was there—her nasal voice pierced through the party noise like a knife through butter. A rusty knife.

My friends and I huddled out of sight behind a handy stack of beach chairs for a while watching the festivities. Butch was clearly visible, his bald head gleaming in the moonlight as he stood in the shallows juggling a bunch of bottles while Lainie and a couple of other girls from the crew watched. He wasn't a very good juggler, but no one seemed to mind. They giggled and applauded every time he dropped one of the bottles.

After a while Madge wandered over to watch too. But she apparently had a short attention span. After a moment she shrugged and splashed out to join a bunch of people who were swimming around and splashing one another farther out in the water. Butch noticed and tossed aside his bottles.

"Splash fight!" he called out, his gruff voice carrying on the night air.

Several people screamed gleefully as he dove in, splashing everyone vigorously by pumping his feet in the water. Lainie and one of the other girls with her wandered back up the beach and sat down on the sand to talk to Donald while everyone else rushed to join in the splash fight.

"Okay, this is pretty pointless," I murmured to Bess and George after a few more minutes. "This party looks like it could go on for quite a while, and it's getting late. We need to get some sleep if we want to figure things out tomorrow."

Bess nodded, stifling a yawn. "Let's head back."

We tiptoed up the beach, heading for the main walkway leading back out to the bungalows. Akinyi's bungalow was the first one we had to pass to get to ours; as we approached it I saw that there was still a light on inside. Then I saw the front door open. A tall, thin figure slipped out and hurried off down the walkway without noticing us watching—but I was pretty sure that tall, thin figure *wasn't* Akinyi.

Bess realized it too and let out a soft gasp. "Hey!" she whispered. "Who's that sneaking out of Akinyi's hut?"

"I'll tell you exactly who it is," George hissed grimly. "It's Vic!"

IT'S A JUNGLE OUT THERE

"What would Vic be doing in Akinyi's bungalow?" Bess whispered. "It's almost midnight!"

"Come on, let's follow him." Without waiting for an answer, I hurried up the steps and along the walkway. Glancing over my shoulder, I saw my friends following.

We tracked Vic as he hurried along the maze of walkways over the water. The three of us have tracked a few bad guys in our time, so we're pretty good at it. Even so, it almost seemed like Vic might be on to us. A couple of times he paused and peered around into the darkness, forcing us to hide behind anything handy. But then he always kept going, eventually reaching the bungalow he shared with Sydney. After one last glance around, he opened the door and slipped inside.

My friends and I stayed put for a few minutes, but nothing else happened. The lights were all off in the bungalow, and the only things we could hear were fish splashing in the lagoon beneath us and the distant sounds of the crew party farther down the beach.

Finally we gave up and returned to our own bungalow. "Well?" George said, flopping onto the wicker couch in the main room. "What do you think that was all about?"

Bess had tears in her eyes as she shook her head. "All I can say is, if Vic is cheating on Syd—especially with her best friend—MrSilhouette will have to get in line. Because I'll kill Vic myself."

"Right with you, cousin," George agreed.

"Hang on," I said. "Let's not freak out until we know for sure what's happening here. For all we know, he might have forgotten something at Akinyi's when he and Syd were hiding out there earlier, and was just going back to get it."

"At midnight?" George sounded skeptical.

I couldn't blame her. "I don't know," I admitted. "Anyway, it's too late to figure it out tonight. Let's get some sleep and deal with it in the morning."

★ ★ ★

"So, Vic." I fell into step beside Sydney's new husband as he left the breakfast buffet line the next morning. "I guess you and Syd were out and about late last night, huh?" I pasted on what I hoped was an innocent smile. "See, I couldn't sleep and so I went for a walk along the walkways for a while around midnight. I would have sworn I heard the door to your bungalow close when I was passing by. Did you two go for a nice romantic moonlit walk along the beach or something?"

"Nope, wasn't us," Vic replied cheerfully. "Sounds like a cool idea, though—we'll have to try it tonight. But last night Syd and I both went to bed early and slept like logs. Must've had the wrong cabin, Nancy."

"Oh. You're probably right." I maintained my smile until he turned away to help himself to a glass of juice. Then I allowed it to fade. I'd been trying to give Vic the benefit of the doubt. But he wasn't making it easy. We'd seen him with our own eyes last night. Why was he lying about it?

"Ugh. I think another one just got me." George slapped at her arm. "What am I, some kind of mosquito magnet or something? They don't seem to be biting *you*." She glared at Bess.

"I guess you must taste better," Bess said, sounding

distracted. She lifted her foot out of a patch of mud and stared woefully at her sneaker. "Listen, Nancy. What are we hoping to find out here? Because if I'm going to ruin my shoes, I want to know it's for some greater purpose."

"I already told you, remember?" I gingerly pushed aside a low-growing palm with sharp-looking fronds. "We're trying to find the spot where whoever it was shot at our boat yesterday. Maybe that will give us some hints about who it was."

We'd been fighting our way through the jungle north of the resort for about half an hour, though it felt more like three or four days. As soon as we'd left the manicured area around the resort, the landscape had changed drastically. It was buggy and muddy and itchy and just generally unpleasant. My friends and I were already exhausted, not to mention sweaty and dirty from head to toe and, in George's case, covered with mosquito bites.

"What kind of hints are we looking for, exactly?" George asked.

"You know—old-fashioned clues," I said. "Like footprints or whatever."

Bess bit her lip as she glanced down again at her feet. "Well, just know that I've probably already sacrificed a really cute pair of sneakers to the cause. I'm not sure I can save them." She sighed. "At least they weren't superexpensive like those sandals Akinyi wrecked yesterday."

I nodded, recalling the muddy sandals we'd seen in the model's bungalow. "Speaking of footprints, those shoes of hers should make it easy to tell if any prints we find are hers. I doubt many people come out here in high-heeled sandals." I winced as my ankle turned on a root, though I caught myself on the trunk of a nearby tree in time to prevent injury. Unfortunately, that tree trunk happened to be covered in ants, which began swarming and biting my hand with great enthusiasm.

"Do you really think Akinyi could've been the one who shot out our pontoons yesterday?" George asked, smacking herself on the shoulder and watching as I rubbed the ants off in a handy mud puddle.

"I hope not," I admitted. "But it does seem pretty suspicious. Why would she go wandering into the jungle like that? The way she reacted to that fly in the dining room last night, I'm thinking she's not exactly a nature lover."

Bess hopped over a fallen tree branch. "Yeah. Plus she did make us wait before she let us in yesterday even though she knew Syd was frantic," she recalled. "Why would she do that? It's not like she even changed out of her robe while we were waiting. Maybe she was hiding the evidence of what she'd been up to, and just forgot about those shoes until Vic tripped over them."

"That's what I was thinking," I said. "There were all those thumping noises from inside, like she was opening and closing drawers or closet doors." I shook my head. "But listen, we need to keep an open mind here. Akinyi may look kind of suspicious right now, but she's not our only suspect."

"Right," George said. "There's still Butch, for instance."

I nodded. "He could have done the shooting, too, at least as far as we know. He wasn't on the beach when we swam in, remember?"

"Are you sure?" George asked.

"Yeah, I remember that too," Bess said. "There were a couple of cameramen there, but Butch wasn't one of them—I remember thinking I was glad about that, since he probably would have had some obnoxious comment to make."

"Right. He wasn't there, and neither was Madge," I said. "Or Donald or Lainie, for that matter."

"Lainie?" George glanced over at me. "Don't tell me she's on the list."

I shrugged, stepping carefully over a swampy-looking spot on the narrow animal track we were following at the moment. "Not really," I said. "But it does seem a teensy bit suspicious that she's just suddenly there flirting with Bo all the time, doesn't it? Plus she disappeared at a critical moment right before the waterfall incident yesterday."

Bess crinkled her nose. "Are you saying you think she could've climbed up, loosened that stone, and then come back in time to watch Bo fall?" she asked skeptically. "But how would she know one of those guys would even climb up there?"

"Maybe she put the idea in Butch's head," I said. "Or maybe it was just a coincidence that she left at that particular time. Look, I'm not saying she's a strong suspect. I'm just saying we shouldn't rule anybody out, okay?"

"I hear you," George said with a sigh. "And I agree. I don't think any of us wants to believe Vic could be involved. Or even Akinyi."

Bess nodded. "True."

We were silent for a few minutes, focused on fighting both our own thoughts and the choking, merciless jungle. Finally, though, the trees and undergrowth began to thin up ahead.

"I think we're almost to the water," Bess panted, pushing forward through some palm fronds.

I felt my foot squish down in an extra-deep mud puddle, but I didn't care. "Come on, let's see where we are."

A moment later we stepped out into a beautiful

little cove. A pristine white sand beach curved in around the shallows, with tiny waves patting the sand with each pulse of the tide. Due to the uneven coastline, the spot lay out of sight of the resort, making it feel as isolated as a deserted island.

"Wow, this is gorgeous!" Bess breathed, turning on her heel to scan the scene. "It looks like something out of a movie."

"Check this out, you guys," George said from somewhere behind us.

Turning, I saw that she was standing beside a stack of large wooden crates. They were sitting at the edge of the jungle, partly obscured by a low-growing palm, which was why I hadn't noticed them at first.

"What's that?" I asked, heading over.

"Don't know." George knocked on the side of one of the crates. "Should we see if we can open it?"

I'd just noticed the Oro Beach Resort logo stamped on the side. "Better not," I said. "We must still be on resort property. I doubt these boxes have anything to do with our case."

Bess was shading her eyes, peering off into the jungle near the crates. "Look, guys," she called. "I think we took the scenic route getting here. That looks like a real trail, doesn't it?"

She was right. Leading off the far side of the cove was a well-worn dirt track, easily wide enough for the truck or ATV that must have carried the crates out there from the main part of the resort.

"Maybe they run diving expeditions out of here or something," I said. "The gear could be in those crates."

"Why would they bring people way out here?" George sounded skeptical.

"Who knows?" Bess shrugged. "But unless you think the Oro Beach Resort is somehow involved in sabotaging Syd's life, I don't think we should let ourselves get too distracted by worrying about stuff like that."

"You're probably right," I agreed. "The real question is, could someone have shot out our pontoons from here?"

Bess squinted out across the sparkling waters of the lagoon. "I think so," she said, pointing straight out across the water. "I'm pretty sure our boat was right about there when we got hit."

"I think you're right," I agreed. "Unfortunately, I don't think we're going to find any useful footprints here. The tide would've washed them away since yesterday."

"There are some back here," George was still back near the crates, though she'd taken a few steps away to peer at the muddy ground just beyond the edge of the sand. "A bunch, actually."

"Anything that looks like a Louboutin sandal?" Bess asked, hurrying over.

George rolled her eyes. "If you mean something with a heel, then no. I don't see anything like that."

"The shooter wouldn't have been hanging around back there by those crates," I said. "He or she would have been out closer to the water. Although now that I think about it, I'm not sure he or she would've been in a spot like this at all. It would make much more sense to hide in the jungle to stay out of view from the water."

Bess let out a pained sigh. "So you want us to go searching for footprints in the jungle?"

I sighed too. "No. We could search all day and not find anything in there. We might as well just head back." I shot a look at the dirt trail, relieved that at least the walk home would be a little easier than the trek out here.

"I can't believe it," George joked as she smacked at another mosquito on her leg. "Nancy Drew isn't cowed by the most hardened and nasty of criminals. But the tropical jungle might just have her beat!"

I grinned weakly, not about to deny it. "Come on," I said. "I'm ready for a nice, hot shower. Let's just keep our fingers crossed that this thing really does lead back to the resort."

As it turned out, it did. The dirt road was rutted and rough in spots, but it still made for a much, much easier time than fighting our way through the jungle.

The trip that had taken us more than forty-five minutes on the way out was more like fifteen or twenty on the return trip.

"Here we are," Bess said as we caught our first glimpse of civilization up ahead. "Home again."

We hurried forward. When we emerged from the tree line, George looked around in surprise. "Hey," she said. "Are we in the right place?"

For a second I felt disoriented too. We had stepped out into a sort of grassy clearing dotted with about a dozen rustic wooden cabins. Then I caught a glimpse of the thatched roof of the main building over the top of a hedge.

"This must be another section we haven't seen yet—maybe less expensive rooms than the ones over the water, or staff housing or something." At that moment, I heard the slam of a door at the far edge of the cabin area. Glancing that way, I was just in time to catch the back of a familiar strawberry blond head hurrying off toward the beach.

"Hey, that looked like Lainie," Bess said at the same moment. "I'd recognize her amazing head of hair anywhere. And I love that cool French braid she has it in right now! I wonder if she'd show me how to do that."

"Forget your hair," George said, stepping forward. "Now that we know where Lainie's staying, maybe we should check it out." She shot me a look. "Like you said, everyone's a suspect, right?"

I *had* said that. But even as I followed my friends toward the cabin Lainie had just left, I had my doubts. Maybe it was time to face the facts. Other than Butch, who still deserved a spot high on the suspect list, there were exactly two other people who had earned a place there through their recent behavior. Unfortunately, one of them was Sydney's best friend, and the other was her husband. How was I ever going to face Sydney if it turned out Vic had been behind the trouble all along? More importantly, how was Sydney herself ever going to face her future?

I was so deep in thought that I fell behind as my friends reached Lainie's cabin and peered in through a window. But Bess's loud gasp snapped me out of it.

"What?" I hurried forward to join them. At first I didn't see anything unusual. The view through the window showed a fairly ordinary-looking bedroom, smaller and less luxurious than ours but still quite nice. The bed was neatly made and the floor swept, though it was obvious that someone was staying there thanks to the sweater dropped carelessly on a chair and a pair of flip-flops over near the door. There were also a few personal items on the bedside table— a hairbrush, a paperback book, a framed photo . . .

"Hey," I said as I saw the photo, which showed a smiling young woman with dark curly hair hugging a cute dog. "Do we have the wrong room? That's not Lainie in the picture."

"Yes it is," Bess said. "Look at the face. It's her—but with totally different hair."

"So what?" George shrugged. "People change their hair all the time. Don't you remember that curling iron phase you went through back in middle school?"

"Or it could be a picture of a relative," I put in. "Twin sister, maybe?"

Bess was shaking her head. "No, it's her," she insisted. "Can't you see that mole?"

My eyesight is pretty good, but Bess has to be part eagle or something. When I squinted, I saw that she was right. The girl in the picture had the same distinctive mole on her chin as Lainie.

"Never mind the picture," Bess said, nudging me with her shoulder. "Do you guys see what else is in there? Check out the bathroom."

For the first time I noticed that the bathroom door was slightly ajar. Just inside on the counter lay a mop of strawberry blond—a wig!

"Oh, my gosh!" George covered her mouth with one hand. "Are you guys thinking what I'm thinking?"

"Only if you're thinking MrSilhouette could be

female," I said grimly. "I suppose we should have thought of that. After all, crazy stalkers come in both genders. Come to think of it, maybe that's even why she signed the notes and stuff the way she did. It was capital *M*, small *r*, capital *S* all run together, remember?"

Bess nodded. "I get it. MrS. It kind of looks like Mrs. rather than Mr. . . ."

"Hey," someone said from just behind us. "What are you doing at my cabin?"

DEAD ENDS AND DISCUSSIONS

We whirled around, already stammering out excuses. Lainie stood there looking confused.

"Um, I mean, oh, is this your cabin?" I babbled. "We were just passing by and were wondering what they looked like inside. What a coincidence!"

Lainie crossed her arms over her chest, narrowing her eyes. "Come on, you guys," she said. "Bo already told me you're, like, detectives or something. But why are you snooping around here?"

Oops! It looked like we were busted. Deciding to take advantage of the chance encounter to try to surprise a confession out of her, I took a deep breath.

"I'll tell you why," I said. "But first, I want you to tell us something, Lainie. Are you MrSilhouette?"

Lainie looked more confused than ever. "Mr. Who?" she said. "What are you talking about?"

"Come on," George put in. "We saw the wig. Have you been stalking Syd all this time? Doing all the bad stuff?"

"Me?" By now, Lainie's expression had gone from confused to downright astonished. If she was acting, she was awfully good at it. "You mean all the accidents and problems that have been happening during this shoot, like the loose rock at the pool and the wrecked honeymoon bungalow and whatever? Of course I didn't do any of that! Why would I?"

"Because you've been obsessed with Sydney for the past couple of years?" Bess put in. "Because you didn't want her to marry Vic?"

Lainie held up both hands. "Hang on," she said. "You've totally lost me. Why would I care if Sydney and Vic got married? Hey, their wedding landed me a job, okay?"

"It did?" I said. "So you mean you just got hired on for this special? You didn't work on *Daredevils* before that?"

Lainie shook her head. "Before this I was doing temp work for a bunch of low-budget plays and stuff."

"Was that in New York?" Bess asked.

"Nope. L.A." Lainie shrugged. "Look, I don't know why you guys suddenly decided I was, like, some criminal mastermind or something. But I can tell you, it wasn't me. I never met or even heard of Sydney before about two months ago when I got hired for this gig. And the only place I'd ever seen Vic was on TV."

"But the wig," George blurted out. "MrSilhouette sent Syd those photos of the back of a bald head. . . ."

At that, Lainie's face suddenly sort of crumpled and went red. I perked up. Was she about to confess?

"Okay," she muttered. "Now I get it, sort of. Although I wouldn't exactly say I'm technically bald. Not anymore."

With that, she pulled off her strawberry blond braided hair, revealing a head of wispy dark hair barely two inches long. Nope. Definitely not bald, at least not like in that photo. . . .

"I'm a cancer survivor," Lainie said, her voice shaking a little as she stood there with her wig in one hand and her wisps blowing in the light breeze. "I finished my last round of chemo right before I got this job. That's why I wear wigs—I lost all my hair during the treatment."

"Oh!" Bess took a step forward, touching her gently on the arm. "Lainie, we're so sorry. We didn't know—and when we saw the wig, and knowing what we know about Sydney's stalker being someone bald, we just thought—"

"It's okay," Lainie broke in, her voice stronger now. "I haven't told anyone here about it, so there's no way you could have known. I—I just didn't want anyone to feel sorry for me or treat me any differently, you know?"

"Like Bo," I said, suddenly realizing that this explained that odd little scene by the pool. "That's why you got so upset when he tried to pull you into the water yesterday."

She looked surprised for a moment. Then she nodded. "Right," she said. "He's cool and we're having fun together and all. But I just wasn't ready to tell him. Especially not in front of all those people and the cameras and everything."

I exchanged a look with my friends. "Don't worry," I said. "We won't tell a soul."

Bess nodded. "Your secret is safe with us."

"So how do you guys know Lainie was telling the truth, the whole truth, and nothing but?" George said a few minutes later as the three of us made our way along a shelly path leading toward the beach. "Maybe we should double-check her story."

Bess rolled her eyes. "Come on," she said. "The

wig thing and her weird behavior by the pool were the only reasons to suspect her in the first place. Besides, you saw her—there's no way she could have taken that bald lagoon photo just a few days ago and already have her hair grow out that much."

"Bess is right." I bit my lip. "Still, something's kind of bugging me about that whole scene. I'm just not sure what it is."

Bess raised an eyebrow. "You mean you think Lainie might have done it after all?"

"No, I'm pretty sure she's innocent," I said. "But still . . ."

At that moment the sound of Sydney's voice came drifting toward us from somewhere ahead. We were too far away to hear what she was saying, but she sounded pretty hysterical.

"Uh-oh." Bess put on a burst of speed. "Sounds like something's wrong."

"Again," George added.

We hurried down the path and emerged onto the strip of sand at the base of the stairs that led up to the bungalow walkways. Sydney was standing at the top of the stairway, tears streaming down her face as she babbled almost incoherently. Donald was there too, ineffectively trying to soothe her as Butch stood by filming it all with a slight smirk on his broad face.

"Syd!" Bess rushed up to her, taking the steps two at a time. "What's going on?"

Sydney whirled to face us as George and I hurried up the steps as well. "It's Vic!" she wailed. "He was supposed to meet me back in our bungalow for a nice catered lunch. We were both looking forward to it all day. But I've been waiting twenty minutes and he still hasn't showed!"

George looked relieved. "Oh, is that all?" she said. "Look, Syd, I get why you're upset. But this is Vic we're talking about, remember? Mr. ADHD himself? He probably just lost track of the time."

"That's what I thought." Sydney choked back a sob. "I mean, I spent the whole morning in the spa with Akinyi, so it wouldn't be that surprising that he'd forget without me around to remind him. But he's not answering his cell, and Kinnie and I have been searching the whole resort and can't find him anywhere!"

I couldn't tell whether she was upset because Vic missed their romantic lunch, or if she was afraid he was late because something had happened to him. Either way, she was pretty freaked out.

"Don't worry, Syd," I said. "We'll track him down. Now, when was the last time you—"

"Hello, hello!" Vic's breathless voice burst out from the sand below. "Sorry I'm late. Whoa, Syd, you okay, love?" He leaped up the steps three at a time.

"Vic!" Sydney shrieked, flinging herself at him. "Thank goodness! I thought I'd never see you again."

"Sorry, babe." Vic's eyes widened in surprise as he gently stroked her red hair. "Oh, man, I'm really sorry. I totally didn't mean to upset you. I was playing poker with the guys over at Jamal's bungalow and I guess we lost track of time."

Sydney buried her face in his chest. "It's okay," she said, her voice muffled by his shirt. "Just don't do that to me again, all right?"

"I promise." Vic squeezed her tight and planted a kiss on the top of her head.

Sydney seemed mollified by his apology. Her expression was already clearing, and her sniffles getting further apart. But I wasn't really buying Vic's story—especially since I'd just noticed that his shoes were muddy.

"Come on, you two." Donald started waving his hands around, shooing the couple farther down the walkway. In all the excitement, I'd almost forgotten he was still there. "You don't want your food getting cold." He smiled and shrugged. "Well, any colder than it already is, anyway."

Vic and Sydney chuckled and headed arm in arm down the walkway toward their bungalow. Butch followed, filming the whole time, and Donald trailed along behind him.

That left me alone with my friends at the top of the steps. "Did you guys see Vic's shoes?" I asked as soon as I was sure the others were out of earshot.

"His shoes? No, why?" George asked.

I quickly explained about the mud. Bess's eyes widened. She glanced down at the planked walkway and nodded grimly as she spotted one of the muddy prints he'd left.

"I can tell you one thing," she said. "He didn't get them muddy in Jamal's bungalow! So where was he, and what was he really doing all this time?"

"Good question." I shrugged. "At least Akinyi doesn't seem to be involved this time. Syd said they spent the whole morning together, remember?"

"Unless she and Vic are working together," George pointed out darkly. "Don't forget it was her cabin we caught Vic leaving last night."

"That's true," I said reluctantly. "I still just hate to think there could be anything—"

I cut myself off as a piercing scream rang out over the entire area, echoing off the lagoon. "That sounded like Syd!" Bess cried, already running down the walkway.

"Hey," someone called from the direction of the beach. "What's going on?"

Glancing that way, I saw that Jamal and Bo had just appeared at the edge of the sand carrying tennis rackets. But I didn't bother stopping to explain anything to them as I took off after my friends.

When we reached the honeymoon hut we found Donald dancing around helplessly on the porch. "Oh, it's terrible!" he exclaimed. "Why do these things keep happening? It's like this wedding is cursed. . . ."

Ignoring him, I pushed past and burst into the bungalow. Sydney and Vic were seated at a small table covered in a white linen cloth. A pretty, young waitress stood nearby, her eyes wide and a napkin pressed against her mouth. Butch was there too, his mouth ajar and his camera pointing at the floor. All four of them were staring in horror at the gourmet lunch spread out on the table. Or, to be specific, at Vic's plate. Vic was holding a knife and fork over a juicy piece of steak, watching in horror as dozens of wriggling maggots came squirming out of the cut in the meat!

11

UNPLEASANT SURPRISES

"Oh, gross!" George exclaimed, backing away. Bess gulped audibly. Despite her super-feminine appearance, she isn't easily grossed out. But even she looked a little green around the gills as she stared down at the squirming mass on Vic's plate. "Wh-what happened?" she asked.

"Oh, my gosh," Sydney was in tears. She'd pushed her chair back as far as it would go without crashing into the wall behind her, and had both hands over her mouth. "Oh, my gosh!"

Vic seemed kind of stunned too. "I just cut into my steak, and those things started pouring out!" he exclaimed.

I averted my eyes from the maggots, not wanting to get distracted by my own churning stomach. There was no doubt about it. MrSilhouette had struck again.

"Where did this steak come from?" I asked the waitress, who was cowering back against the wall.

She blinked at me so blankly that for a moment I feared she might not speak English. But finally she answered.

"Um, the kitchen?" she said. "At least I guess it did—I didn't bring it. I was here setting up the dishes and stuff. One of the glasses had some dust in it, and when I came out of the bathroom from rinsing it off, the tray with the rest of the food was here. So I just went ahead and set it up."

"Come on." I glanced at my friends. "Let's go talk to the cook."

Jamal and Bo had arrived by then. Leaving them to comfort Sydney and Vic, we hurried back out the door.

"Is she okay?" Donald asked as soon as we emerged onto the porch. "Sydney, I mean."

"She'll survive," George said, pushing past him.

The three of us hurried down the walkways and back into the resort's central area. By asking a passing employee, we found our way to the main kitchen, which was located in a separate building just across from the dining room. When we got there, we tracked down the head chef, a stout man with a strong Jamaican accent. He seemed genuinely shocked when he heard about what had happened.

"No!" he cried in dismay. "But I cooked that steak myself—medium rare, just as Mr. Valdez requested!"

"He did?" I said. "You mean Vic ordered that lunch from you personally?"

The chef shook his head. "No, not personally. I got the order from the front office."

"Okay," I said. "Then who took it out to the bungalow? The waitress who was there said she didn't know who brought it over."

"I don't know either." The chef looked sheepish. "I was about to call in Kara from the dining room to deliver it. But that infernally annoying director woman came in and started complaining about her coffee being cold just as I finished loading the tray." He frowned. "By the time I turned around again, the tray was gone. I suppose I assumed either Kara had come along and grabbed it, or Louisa had returned from the honeymoon hut to pick it up."

"Thanks," I said thoughtfully. "You've been very helpful."

My friends followed as I left the kitchen. "Is that all you're going to ask him?" George demanded, hurrying to catch up. "Don't you think that guy could be a suspect?"

"Not really." I shrugged. "Why would he plant maggots in his own food? It would only get him fired, plus there's no way someone like that could've been responsible for the stuff that happened back in River Heights. But it *is* kind of suspicious that Madge turned up right at that moment. Just because Lainie didn't turn out to be MrSilhouette, it doesn't necessarily mean we were wrong about it being a woman."

Bess looked intrigued. "So should we go find Madge?" She shuddered. "I have to admit, I'm not looking forward to questioning her."

"I know what you mean." I squared my shoulders. "But somebody has to do the dirty work."

We set out in search of the assistant director. But we'd barely made it ten steps away from the kitchen when I heard a commotion behind us. Turning, I saw Bo, Jamal, and Akinyi hurrying along the path toward the dining room.

Bo spotted us first. "Hey! Come on to lunch, you guys." He grabbed me by the arm. "We want everyone there to cheer up Vic and Syd."

Jamal nodded and shuddered. "You know, because of what just happened."

"Yes, please come," Akinyi added. "We can't let this ruin their honeymoon!"

I wanted to protest, but they didn't give me the chance. Bess, George, and I were swept along as they rushed on toward the dining room.

"Oh, well," Bess murmured as we all took our seats around one of the big tables. "Maybe they're right. Syd can probably use all the moral support she can get right now."

"She could use an answer to this case a lot more," I muttered back. Still, I supposed Bess had a point. Besides, maybe I could use this opportunity to kill two birds with one stone. "Hey, Jamal," I said, putting on a jovial, joking tone as I turned to Vic's friend, who was sitting directly across from me. "I'm surprised you even want to cheer up Vic at this point. He said he totally killed you at poker."

"He did?" Jamal sounded confused. "When was that? Because Vic and I haven't—"

"Go on, Jamal," Akinyi broke in, giving Jamal an elbow to the ribs and a pointed look. "Just man up and admit it, all right? Vic took you to school in poker today."

Jamal blinked. "Oh!" he said. "Um, that's right. Sorry, guess I'm just a little sensitive about losing all that money, you know? Why can't a dude with a big-shot TV career ahead of him cut me a break and let me win?" He chuckled, though I couldn't help noticing it sounded a little forced.

"Yeah!" Bo put in loudly. "I know what you mean. Vic took all my dough too. Let's make him throw us a big beach party tonight to make up for it. What do you say?"

"So if you guys were playing poker all morning, what was with the tennis rackets?" I asked, still trying to sound casual. "I saw you two with them when you came running after Sydney screamed."

Jamal and Bo traded a look. "Oh, that," Bo said with a shrug. "Yeah, we were going to try to get a few sets in before lunch. We were just heading for the courts when we heard Syd, so we turned around and came back."

He sounded pretty sincere. But I wasn't sure I believed him. Vic had been rushing and out of breath when he'd arrived to apologize to Sydney. Would Jamal and Bo really have had time to get their rackets and head over to the tennis courts in the same amount of time it had taken him to race to find her? My hunch-o-meter was telling me they were lying—that there hadn't been any poker game that morning at all. But if so, why were they covering for Vic? Was it just a loyalty thing, an automatic benefit of male friendship? Or was something else going on that they were all in on together?

"Vic, my man!" Bo shouted at that moment, breaking me out of my thoughts. "There's the happy couple. Come on over."

Looking up, I saw that Vic had just entered with Sydney clinging to his arm. The two of them headed toward us, and after that I threw myself into cheering them up along with everyone else.

Even so, a little part of my mind kept worrying at this newest question like a dog with a bone. Why had Jamal, Bo, and Akinyi lied to me just now? What were they—and Vic—trying to hide?

I was just licking the last bit of pineapple ice cream off my spoon when Madge stomped into the dining room. "Uh-oh," Jamal murmured, rolling his eyes. "Here comes trouble."

"You two," Madge spat out disagreeably when she reached the table, stabbing a red-tipped finger at Vic and Sydney. "And you and you." She turned to include Akinyi and Bo. "Go get changed. We're filming those pool scenes in half an hour, remember?"

"Oh, right." Akinyi sat back in her chair and yawned. "You know, when I agreed to come here, I didn't know it was going to be a *working* vacation."

I couldn't tell whether she was joking or not. Sydney seemed to think so, since she chuckled and nudged her friend on the shoulder. "Come on, Kinnie," she said, standing up. "Let's go get beautiful for the cameras."

That made Akinyi crack a smile. "Don't be silly,"

she said, standing up herself. "We are *always* beautiful, remember?"

They giggled like schoolgirls at that. I suspected it was some kind of private joke—with all that had happened lately, it was easy to forget that they were best friends.

Soon the celebrities had left to get ready for the filming and Jamal had wandered off. That left me and my friends alone at the table.

"So," George said, picking at the remains of her dessert. "What now?"

"Hang on." I'd just noticed that Madge hadn't left the room yet. She was standing by the hostess stand talking on her cell phone. "This could be my chance to question you-know-who." I stood and winked at my friends. "If I'm not back in fifteen minutes, tell my dad I loved him, okay?"

"Good luck," Bess said with a shudder.

"If she kills you and eats you, can I have your car?" George added.

I stuck out my tongue at her. Then I hurried toward Madge, reaching her just as she hung up her phone.

"Excuse me," I said before she could hurry off. "I have something to ask you."

"Well, go ahead and ask already—no need to make an announcement about it. I have things to do." Madge sounded impatient, barely bothering to glance at me as she scrolled through the menu on her phone.

I took a deep breath. "I'm sure you've heard about what happened with Vic's lunch earlier," I said. "I talked to the chef who made that steak, and he said you came in just as he was setting out the tray with that steak on it. I was just wondering if you saw anything suspicious while you were in the kitchen."

Okay, that wasn't exactly what I was wondering. But I figured seeing how she answered might give me some hints.

Madge finally looked straight at me, scowling. But her anger didn't seem to be directed at me.

"That idiot Donald!" she burst out. "I should just fire that pathetic twerp already. Not only is he completely incapable of fetching me a cup of coffee that's actually hot, but he's too big a wimp even to go complain to the kitchen about it! Like I don't have anything better to do!" She rolled her eyes. "That's why I made him play waitress so the actual waitress could make me some fresh coffee. And it sounds like he couldn't even do *that* right, if he let someone at that food. . . ." She trailed off in a few muttered swear words, then stomped off.

I couldn't help being a little surprised. Sure, Donald was pretty mild-mannered. But he'd always seemed very efficient and capable to me. Why would he suddenly be too timid to confront the kitchen staff? Was this just Madge trying to create some kind of alibi?

I returned and told my friends what little I'd learned. "So Donald was the one who delivered that tray?" Bess said.

"That's what Madge says." I shrugged. "Do you guys think it's possible he could be the one who tampered with the steak?"

"But why?" George asked. "What's the motive? Think he's working with Butch or something?"

"I suppose it's possible." I tapped the edge of the table with my fingers. "Donald certainly had the access to pull off all the pranks so far, though it's hard to imagine him having the gumption." I let out a sigh of frustration. "I can't believe we were worried about not having any suspects when we first got here. Now it seems like everyone's a suspect except the three of us—"

"And Sydney," Bess put in.

I nodded. "And Sydney," I agreed. "Anyway, there are plenty of suspects but none of them makes sense. Are we really dealing with MrSilhouette, or is someone just using that bit of Syd's history to mess with her?"

"That would mean it'd have to be someone who knows about her stalker in the first place," George pointed out. "Would someone like Madge or Donald have that kind of knowledge?"

"I'm not sure. They might, after what happened before the wedding." I stood up. "In any case, I think we'd better get over to the pool and keep an eye on things."

When we reached the main pool area, we found Madge there pacing back and forth along the edge of the water. Butch and one of the other TV camera operators were standing nearby, along with the still photographer we'd seen earlier. Lainie and a few other assorted crew members were also there, along with a couple of resort employees who were busy passing out water and such. I also spotted Jamal; he was lounging on a pool chair sipping a soda and watching the action.

"Come on, let's sit over here out of the way," I told my friends, leading them over to some lounge chairs near where Jamal was sitting, well out of what I assumed would be camera range. Jamal saw us and raised one hand in a lazy wave, but made no effort to come over.

Just as we sat down, Bo, Akinyi, and Vic wandered into view from the direction of the bungalows. "It's about time," Madge snapped, hurrying over to them. "Where's Sydney?"

"She'll be here in a minute," Vic said, sounding

distracted as he glanced around the pool area. "She can't find that blue bikini she was supposed to wear for the shoot, so she's tearing up the bungalow looking for it."

"What?" Madge squawked. "Look, we're supposed to be on a schedule here. . . ."

Vic ignored her, brushing past her as his eyes locked on me. He rushed straight toward where my friends and I were sitting.

"Nancy, there you are," he said when he reached us. "I need to talk to you privately. Now."

"Um, okay." I stood up. What was this all about? Could it have anything to do with his mysterious behavior earlier? Or was he just anxious to hear whether I'd made any progress on the case?

Before I could find out one way or the other, Donald rushed into the pool area, his thin face a mask of anxiety. "Vic!" he called out. "It's Sydney!"

Vic turned, looking impatient. "What about her?"

"I just saw her," Donald panted, his voice shaking. "She was running toward the lap pool, and she was crying pretty hard. . . ."

Vic didn't need to hear any more. "Uh-oh, what now?" he muttered as he took off in the direction Donald was pointing.

"Come on," I said to my friends.

We all took off after him. The lap pool was located a short distance away from the main pool area past the large gym building. The pool itself was about six feet deep, rectangular and fairly plain compared to the other two pools on the property, though its bottom and sides were lined with attractive tiles in various shades of red and brown.

I was right behind Vic when we reached the lap pool's small courtyard. What had he been about to tell me? Considering all that had happened, my heart was in my throat and my mind was filled with terrible possibilities. What if he really had gotten involved in some kind of secret romance with Akinyi—and Sydney had just found out?

No, that couldn't be it, I told myself. It just didn't make sense. Whoever was doing this wasn't just trying to break Vic and Sydney up. He or she was trying to hurt them—especially Vic. There had just been too many close calls to imagine it could be anyone other than the real MrSilhouette this time. The question was, who was MrSilhouette?

We skidded to a stop at the edge of the lap pool. My mind was so busy turning over the facts of the case that it took me a moment to register what I was seeing.

There, lying facedown at the bottom of the pool, was a slim, pale figure with reddish hair, dressed in a blue bikini. And she wasn't moving.

"Syd!" Vic screamed, racing toward the edge.

QUESTIONS AND ANSWERS

"**N**o!" I shouted at almost the same moment, grabbing at Vic. "Vic, stop. Don't jump in there!"

Vic didn't seem to hear me. Most of the rest of the group from the other pool had arrived behind us by now, and a few of them let out screams or exclamations as they spotted the still figure at the bottom of the lap pool. But the only one who reacted to my words was Butch. He reached out and grabbed Vic by the arm just in time to stop him from hurtling over the edge of the pool.

"Let me go!" Vic shouted, fighting frantically against the burly cameraman's grip. "I have to save Syd!"

"Save me?" repeated Sydney, wandering into view behind the others. She looked radiant in an emerald green swimsuit that set off her flaming red hair. "From what?"

Vic goggled at her, going limp in Butch's grasp. "Sydney?" he gasped out. "But—but I thought . . ."

He looked as confused as I'd ever seen him. Actually, just about everyone looked confused. Murmurs rose up from the onlookers.

"What's going on, Nancy?" Akinyi spoke up.

"I'm just working on that question myself." I kicked a handy pebble into the water, watching carefully for anything odd to happen as it hit the water. But it merely plunked in and sank. "Okay, looks like it's not electrified. . . ."

"Huh?" Vic said. Butch had let go by now, and Vic had both arms wrapped around Sydney, who still looked perplexed.

I glanced around and spotted a long-handled pool net leaning against a wall nearby. Grabbing it, I stepped to the edge of the pool.

"Okay, I'm not sure what's going to happen," I said. "But I suspect there's some kind of trap here, so you all might want to stay back just in case."

Using the net, I reached down and poked at the "body" on the bottom of the pool. As soon as I moved the figure a few inches, its hair detached from the rest of it and floated upward.

"Hey!" Lainie cried. "That's my wig!" Then she slapped a hand over her mouth and glanced around. "Oops."

"Wig?" Bo repeated.

I ignored Lainie, though everyone else turned to stare. It wasn't easy to make the long, thin handle of the pool net do what I wanted. But finally I poked the hairless figure at the bottom of the pool hard enough to make it flip over. That revealed its blank, contoured face.

"It's a mannequin!" Bess realized. "Like the ones in some of the shops here."

"Exactly like one of those," I said. Then I gasped, pointing as there was a sudden flash of movement in the water. "Look!"

Several spiny reddish-brown fish had just darted out from the shelter they'd found beneath the mannequin. They immediately swarmed the end of the net and started attacking it.

"Whoa!" One of the resort employees had stepped forward for a better look. Now he took a quick step back, his expression alarmed. "Those are lionfish!"

"What's a lionfish?" Madge demanded.

The employee shook his head. "Terribly venomous," he said, waving his hands around. "It is a good thing that is only a mannequin in there. If any real person had gone into that water and disturbed them, they surely would have attacked! Very serious!"

Bo let out a low whistle. "Okay, but this pool is way far from the lagoon," he said. "So how'd those things get in there?"

I was pretty sure I knew. And when I turned and scanned the onlookers, what I saw confirmed my suspicions. Donald was sidling off to one side, unnoticed by anyone else so far.

"It was Donald," I said, pointing. "Somebody grab him!"

Bo and Jamal looked confused. But when Donald made a break for it, dashing for the nearest gap in the fence surrounding the lap pool, they leaped after him and grabbed him.

"Let me go!" Donald yelled, kicking at them. But he was no match for the two much larger, stronger guys, and after a moment he seemed to give up. "I did it all for you, Sydney!" he cried, twisting around to gaze at her. "We were meant to be together!"

Sydney blinked, looking startled. "What?"

I marched over to Donald. He didn't even seem to notice me coming. His full attention was focused on Sydney. That meant it was no trouble at all for me to reach over and yank his floppy brown hair right off his head, revealing his gleaming bald scalp.

Bess gasped. "A wig!"

"Sydney," I said grimly, "meet MrSilhouette."

"Okay, Nancy." Akinyi tapped her water glass with a spoon. "It's been hours since the police took Donald away, and I think we're all dying to know. How did you figure out it was him? That he was MrSilhouette all along?"

I'd just taken my seat in the dining room. Glancing down the long table, I caught Sydney's eye. She gave me a barely perceptible nod and smile. She and Vic had been with me, Bess, and George at the local police station for most of the afternoon, so of course they knew the whole story already. But I couldn't blame the others for being curious. Nearly everyone connected with the filming had gathered together for dinner, and most of them were now staring at me curiously.

"It was the steak thing," I said, raising my voice enough to make sure everyone could hear me even at the adjoining tables where the crew was seated. "Well, mostly that. Lainie kind of helped too."

I turned to smile at the makeup artist, who looked confused. "I did?" she said.

"See, Donald never really made it past the least-likely group on the suspect list," I explained. "That was partly because of his mild-mannered, professional, and helpful act. But it was also because of his floppy head of hair."

"Oh!" Akinyi nodded. "I see. We knew that MrSilhouette was bald. . . ."

"And so we didn't seriously consider anyone who had tons of hair like Donald did. Or seemed to," I finished for her. Then I glanced at Bess and George. "That's what started bugging me after we talked to Lainie. We really hadn't considered that if MrSilhouette was hanging around, he could easily be disguising his baldness with a wig."

"Duh," George said. "Seems so obvious now, doesn't it?"

"So it was really Donald causing all the trouble?" Bo asked.

"Right. Except for the stuff Candy did," George put in. "She was guilty too. But Donald did everything else. The jet fuel, that big light that almost fell on Vic right before the wedding . . ."

Bess nodded. "He also managed to frame Akinyi and Jamal by planting that so-called evidence in their hotel rooms," she said. "And he set up Pandora by giving her the note suggesting she perform that Native American knife ritual, pretending it was from the director."

"He also sent most of the e-mails and texts," I added. "And the fake RSVP card, and a bunch of

141

other stuff. He was the one who convinced Butch to try to get Vic to climb up that pool waterfall—I actually noticed the two of them talking together right before it all happened, before Bo talked to him, but I didn't put two and two together then. And of course, Donald was the one who tampered with Vic's steak after making sure Madge came in at just the right moment to distract the cook so he could snag the tray." I sighed. "Like George said, it all seems so clear now, looking back. Donald had the access, the opportunity, and as it turns out, the motive—namely, that he was obsessed with Sydney. But it wasn't until I saw that body in the pool that it all clicked into place."

"But how?" someone called out from the next table.

"I remembered that Vic said Syd couldn't find her blue bathing suit, and I guessed that that was because someone had sneaked in and stolen it to set up some new mischief. And since Donald was the one who came running with that story about seeing Syd crying . . ."

"Which meant it pretty much had to be him who set it up," Vic said, nodding. "But hey, I forgot to ask earlier, Nance—how'd you know to stop me from diving in?"

"Just a guess." I smiled at him, trying not to think about what might have happened if he'd managed to dive into that pool anyway. "You're lucky Butch was close enough to grab you. And that he likes man-handling the talent."

Everyone laughed at that. Even Butch cracked a smile, though he almost immediately let out a snort and pretended to be very busy with his food.

"Anyway," Vic spoke up, "Donald confessed to everything."

"Yeah." George shrugged. "It almost seemed like he was proud of all the chaos he caused."

Sydney shuddered. "At least he should be in jail for a good long time," she said. "Nancy, I'll never be able to thank you enough. I can't tell you what it means to finally be able to go about my life without having to look over my shoulder all the time."

"You're welcome," I replied, thinking of what she'd planned to do if we hadn't solved the case. With any luck, Vic would never have to know how close he'd come to losing her. "I'm just sorry I couldn't figure it out sooner, before your wedding was pretty much spoiled."

"Hey, that reminds me. What about Pandora?" one of Lainie's fellow makeup artists spoke up. "Does this let her off the hook?"

"I can answer that one," Bo spoke up. "I called her just before dinner. She's already been cleared of all charges and allowed to go home."

"Good," I said.

But I wasn't really thinking about Pandora. I was watching Sydney as she turned to smile at Vic. Seeing the look they were giving each other reminded me that even though I'd solved the case, there were still a few loose ends I hadn't managed to tie up. What had Vic been doing in Akinyi's bungalow the night before? Why had the guys all lied about that imaginary poker game? What had all that thumping been from inside Akinyi's bungalow while we were waiting for her to let us in? What had Vic wanted to talk to me about right before Donald sent us all to the lap pool? And come to think of it, there was even that phone call that Vic had hidden from us right after he'd received the photo message from MrSilhouette. He'd said it was from his agent—but was it really?

There were just too many questions left unanswered. I bit my lip as I watched Sydney laugh and tip her face up toward Vic for a kiss, looking more carefree than she had since this whole wedding business had started. I hated the thought that she might be hurt just when she thought she was free to enjoy the rest of her life with the man she loved. . . . But what was I supposed to do about it?

By the time my friends and I headed for our bungalow, those sorts of dark thoughts had given me the beginning of a headache. "Want to take a walk on the beach before bed?" George asked as we reached the steps leading up to the main walkway.

"Not tonight," I said, dragging myself up the steps. "I'm ready to hit the sack. It's been a pretty long day. And we have all week to enjoy the beach and stuff." That was true. After we'd solved the case, *Daredevils* had invited the three of us to stay on at the resort for the rest of the week as a reward.

"Nancy!" someone called from down on the beach.

I looked that way and saw Lainie hurrying toward us. "What is it?" Bess asked her.

"Madge sent me," Lainie said breathlessly. "She needs to see you three about something—now." She grimaced. "And you know Madge. . . . She's over by the beach volleyball net waiting for you."

I groaned. "Way over there?" I complained, glancing up the beach, which was nothing but a shadowy blob in the twilight. "That's, like, a quarter mile down the beach—practically all the way to the jungle!"

"Sorry." Lainie shrugged. "I'm just the messenger."

"We know," Bess told her kindly. Then she glanced at me and George. "What do you say? Want to take that beach walk after all?"

"Might as well," George joked. "Otherwise Madge will probably come drag us out of our beds in the middle of the night and throw us into the lagoon with the lionfish."

"There aren't normally any lionfish in this lagoon," I said automatically. "That guy at the police station said so. Donald admitted he bought them in a nearby town from some black-market guy who caught them somewhere else."

Lainie smiled uncertainly. "So are you coming?"

I hesitated, tempted to blow Madge off. It would be dark soon, and we were all exhausted. And I wasn't really in the mood for the nutty assistant director just then. Not that I ever was, but even the thought of her screechy voice was making my head pound. Surely whatever she wanted to say to us could wait until morning. . . .

Then again, maybe it was easier to go now than to face an extra layer of the assistant director's irritation the next day. "Fine," I muttered, my sense of duty overwhelming my exhaustion. "Let's get it over with. There's a pillow with my name on it back at the bungalow, and I don't want to keep it waiting."

We said good-bye to Lainie and made our way down the beach. It really was pretty that time of the evening, and I was in a slightly better mood by the time the three of us neared the volleyball net. But that mood plummeted again as I glanced around and saw that we were alone.

"Where is she?" I said. "Madge? Hello, Madge? Where are—"

My words were cut off by a large hand clapped over my mouth. I let out a squeak and started to struggle as my arms were pinned to my sides and I was dragged bodily into the jungle. Nearby, I could see two more hooded figures doing the same to my friends.

"Hush!" a voice whispered into my ear. "Please, Nancy. I'm going to let you go, but please don't scream until we get to explain."

Just like that, I felt myself released. "Hey!" I sputtered as soon as my mouth was free. "Who—"

But I didn't need to go on. I'd just turned to find Bo, Vic, and Jamal grinning at us. "Sorry about that," Vic said. "I hope we didn't scare you too much. But we couldn't think of any other way to get you out here without tipping off Madge and the camera crew."

"Huh?" George said, sounding irritated. "What are you talking about?"

Bo checked his watch. "No time to explain now," he said. "Just come on! Our ATVs are hidden right over there."

Twenty minutes later, we found ourselves watching as Vic and Sydney prepared to get married—again—in a private ceremony on the beach in that pretty private cove we'd stumbled upon earlier. It looked a lot different from the last time we'd seen it. The whole place was decorated with tons of flowers and sparkling lights, with tiki torches flickering brightly at water's edge as darkness fell.

"I still can't believe you guys were planning this all along," I told Sydney as Bess and Akinyi fiddled with her hair.

"Not us," Sydney said happily, smoothing the skirt of the plain but elegant white sundress she was wearing. "Just Vic. Well—he had some help." She turned to smile at Akinyi.

Akinyi smiled back and winked. "It wasn't easy keeping the secret from you, Syd." She shot me a look. "Especially with your own private detective snooping around. Plus we had to avoid the cameras at the same time—no easy task."

I grinned. I'd already figured out that this was what Vic had been trying to tell me back by the pool. He'd realized I was starting to get suspicious and wanted to let me in on the secret before I unwittingly ruined all his plans.

Vic heard us talking and glanced up from tying his shoes nearby. He'd already pulled on a snazzy tuxedo over his shorts and T-shirt.

"Yeah, it was a challenge," he agreed, straightening up. "But it was totally worth it. I really wanted to do this again, and do it right this time. No cameras. No extra junk. Just the small romantic ceremony Syd always wanted. The wedding of her dreams." He shot a look at Jamal and Akinyi. "With the people we really care about there to see it this time."

"This all must have something to do with what happened when we knocked on your door yesterday," I said to Akinyi. "We were wondering why you didn't let us in right away—and what all that thumping was about."

Akinyi shrugged. "I had just returned from here," she said, glancing around the cove. "My clothes were covered in mud, plus I had some flowers and other things in my cabin that we hadn't been able to fit in the crates when we brought them out here." She waved a hand at the decorations all around us. "I needed a moment to hide that stuff, and my dirty clothes."

"But you forgot about your sandals," Bess said. "Did you ever manage to get them cleaned up, by the way?"

That brought on a lively discussion between the two of them involving said sandals, which I mostly ignored. I was just happy to finally have the answers to those last, nagging questions. Now I knew why Vic had been sneaking out of Akinyi's bungalow at midnight. They'd been in there—along with Bo and Jamal—making plans after Sydney was asleep. It also explained why the guys had covered for Vic when they hadn't been playing poker that day at all. And that phone call Vic had hidden from sight. None of Sydney's loved ones had been up to anything nefarious after all. They'd been planning this wonderful surprise for her!

Now that everything was out in the open, I couldn't believe I'd ever suspected Vic and Sydney's other friends of all those terrible things. At least I hadn't shared my darker suspicions with Sydney.

"Is everyone ready?" Bo called out, clapping his hands. "If so, would the bride and groom please take your places. . . ."

"Wait, you mean you're doing the ceremony?" George asked him.

Bo grinned. "Sure. I got a certificate from one of those online places." He thumped his broad chest with both fists. "I'm fully accredited!"

"Come on, girls." Sydney grabbed Bess's hand with one of her own and mine with the other. "Time to be bridesmaids."

George groaned. "Again?"

Sydney laughed. "At least you don't have to wear pink this time," she teased. Then she glanced at Akinyi, dropping our hands to grab both of hers. "And at least this time I get to have the maid of honor I wanted."

Akinyi squeezed her hands. "I can't wait."

All traces of my headache gone, I watched as Sydney and Vic stood hand in hand in front of Bo. Sydney looked beautiful and radiantly happy as she gazed up at the man of her dreams. And Vic looked handsome and adoring as he drank in the sight of his beautiful bride as if he never wanted to look away.

The ceremony was simple, short, and perfect. At the end, as bride and groom kissed, I clapped along with everyone else.

"This is great," Bess whispered, beaming at the happy couple. "Sydney finally got the sweet, intimate wedding she always wanted."

George nodded. "And the *Daredevils* viewing audience will never be the wiser."

I smiled as Vic dipped Sydney almost to the sand, making her laugh with delight. "Right," I agreed. "Sometimes secrets can be a *good* thing!"

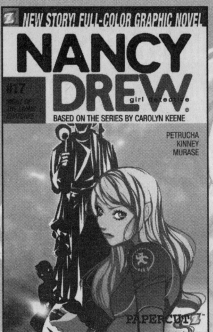